I0564499

THE FARMER'S SECOND CHANCE

A LATER-IN-LIFE ROMANCE

FARMERS OF GOODRICH COUNTY

SHARON A. MITCHELL

ASD PUBLISHING

To Derek who always believed.
You will be missed forever.

CHAPTER 1

After more hugs and touching than Keith was comfortable with, he and Robin drove off in Robin's car. As he helped her into the passenger seat, Keith heard Blair say to his wife, "Why is *he* driving Mom's car?"

Robin pretended she hadn't heard. "That was a lovely meal."

"Yep, it was fine." In the rearview mirror, he watched the twinkling Christmas lights fade in the distance. Blair and his clan had made their place gaudier than a department store in December.

Robin twisted in her seat to look at him. "Just fine?"

What were they talking about? Oh, yeah. "The food was good."

"But?"

"Your son didn't exactly make me feel welcome."

"What did he say?" Robin was ready to take Blair to task if he'd been rude.

"It's not so much what he said. It's what he didn't say. More in how he looked."

"Looked?"

"Glared is more like it."

"Why would my son glare at you?"

"It's a…"

"Don't you dare say it's a guy thing."

Keith shrugged. "Okay, I won't say it, but it is."

"Explain." No one refused Robin when she used that tone.

"It's like he thought I shouldn't be there."

"Nonsense. Becca and her husband were there, and you're her dad, her only relation."

"I don't think Blair cares if I'm Becca's father. It had more to do with the fact that I came with you."

"I told him I asked you to bring me, since I don't like driving in the snow at night."

"Somehow, I don't think that was reason enough for him."

"You don't need a reason. *I* don't need a reason. If I want to catch a ride with a friend, I will."

"He wondered why I was driving your car."

"Did you tell him your pickup tire was low?"

"I'm not in the habit of having to explain myself to anyone."

They rode the next few miles in silence - an easy silence.

Outside, the snow drifted down, not enough to make visibility difficult, but enough to drive with care. Finally, Keith tried again, speaking into the quiet cocoon of the car. "I think I upset Blair."

Robin sighed. Both Keith and Blair could be prickly, and neither backed down. "What did you say?"

"It's not what I said; it's what I *did*. I didn't mean anything by it, but his eyes sent daggers at me when I put my arm around the back of your chair at dinner." He hurried on. "I wasn't trying to get fresh; we were crowded around the table, and I needed to stretch my arm."

Robin grinned. "Fresh?"

"You know what I mean."

"Haven't heard that term since, oh, when we were in high school."

"A decade, or two, or three ago."

"More like four."

"Can't be. You've hardly changed."

Robin rolled her eyes.

"I still remember you in chemistry class."

"*I* remember that you tried to ditch me as your lab partner when Izzy and her family moved to town."

"What can I say? I was smitten with her, and working on labs together was the only way I could get her to talk to me."

They shared a laugh, the kind between long-time friends with history going back forever.

"I remember. She made you work for it, didn't she?"

"You're not kidding. I was desperate. I needed to bind her to me before she noticed the other guys and wouldn't look twice at me."

"When the rest of us all grew up together, anyone new caught our attention."

"Well, Izzy certainly caught mine."

"I noticed." She grinned. "We *all* noticed."

"It was a lot of effort to get her to agree to go out with me, but worth it." Worth every moment of the years they'd had together.

Once again, silence drifted into the car, comfortably filling in the edges.

"But you were different," Keith remembered. "You couldn't wait to get out of Goodrich."

"I had stuff to do."

"And broke Ron's heart when you went to do it."

"Yeah. I felt badly about that later, but at the time, it was something I just had to do. How would I know I wanted to settle down here if I hadn't seen what life was like outside of where I'd grown up?"

"You weren't here to see poor Ron moping around while you were gone."

"It's okay. I made it up to him."

"Yeah. He was like a changed man when you came back home." A quieter man, though.

Keith pulled into Robin's driveway. From habit, he reached for the remote control button hooked to the visor and, without stopping, pulled the car into the garage.

They blinked in the sudden brightness of the garage door opener's light. Keith turned off the engine, and the motor pinged as it cooled down in the unheated garage.

"Are you coming in?" Robin asked.

"No, I don't think I will tonight."

Robin turned to him, a question in her eyes. "I have a bottle of that port you like."

"Tempting, but no. I'll take a rain check, though."

"Tired?" Robin needed an explanation. Usually, when they went out, they spent some time in her living room in front of the fireplace before calling it a night.

"No more than usual for a guy my age." He shifted so his right arm stretched across the back of the seat. "Here's the thing. I keep seeing your son giving me the stink eye if he thinks I'm doing anything with his mother."

"He's my *son*, not my keeper. What I do, or who I see, is none of his business."

"I think he's in protective mode - of both you and his father's memory. Can't fault the boy for that."

"I don't need protection, and he needs to keep his nose out of my business."

"You won't like this, but it's a guy thing. I get it, and Ron would be proud of him for looking out for his mom." He patted Robin's shoulder. "That man raised the boy right."

Robin said nothing. That's not what Blair would say.

CHAPTER 2

S ingle parenting was still new to Blair, and thankfully,
he only did it rarely. Today was one of those days.

His wife, Beth, the school counselor, was in charge
of the annual Christmas concert. She needed to stay at the
school, getting things ready for tonight. Their foster
daughters took the school bus home, and now helped Blair
make supper. "Help" was a questionable word - usually, the
girls were not bad around the kitchen, but this afternoon,
they were too excited to focus on their tasks.

This would be their first concert of any kind. Their birth
parents had never been willing to take their daughters into
town, or participate in anything in the multitude of
communities they'd lived in.

Nine-year-old Randine would get to sit in the audience
with Grandma Robin and Aunt Becca, wearing the new dress
Randine and Beth had picked out.

Fourteen-year-old Friday was part of the crew working
on the concert, dressed in a uniform of black pants and a
white shirt. Her role - to manage the lighting for the
production.

At last, supper was on the table, and eaten in record time. Grateful that Friday was able to help Randine with her hair, Blair loaded the girls into his truck for the drive to the school.

~

K eith Feldman waited patiently for the others to slide into their seats. The seeming courtesy disguised his need to be in the aisle seat without someone crowding him on both sides. His son-in-law, Stan, then his daughter, Becca, settled into their chairs, leaving room for Robin to sit between them and Keith. As Becca passed, he noticed a piece of straw in her hair. Must have been spending time with those darned alpaca creatures that fascinated her so much. Should he mention the straw? No, she'd see that as yet another criticism.

Robin solved the problem. Reaching over, she plucked the offending piece out of Becca's hair, grinning as she held it up. From *her*, Becca took it just fine. It was only her father she got ornery with.

Pretending fascination with his program, Keith took little part in the conversation the other three shared. Although his face showed nothing of his feelings, it was a tad annoying how his daughter opened up to everyone but him. Maybe that was due to Robin; who could resist her?

A tap on his arm got his attention. Randine, the younger of the two girls Robin's son Blair and his wife had taken in, waited, grinning at him. Standing, Keith let the child by, as Robin gave the girl a hug; Becca and Stan moved down a seat to let Randine have the chair in between Robin and Becca.

Robin's charm extended to the child as well.

The lights dimmed, and the audience hushed, as the school's annual Christmas concert began. Although crowds

7

and concerts weren't really his thing, since his hardware store donated the materials to build the sets each year, Izzy had always insisted they make an appearance. After her death, he felt he owed it to her memory to continue attending.

He had thought it would be easier if Becca joined him, but initially, Becca refused to set foot in that high school that she said had caused her so much grief where she'd been bullied and ostracized. Over time, her husband Stan's support, Robin's encouragement, and the warm welcome of the townspeople had thawed Becca's ire.

Never comfortable in a crowd, Keith only half-admitted that it was less daunting when he had people to accompany him. He didn't want to think about how having Robin beside him made it so much easier to sit here.

Although she'd helped with the concert for decades, it never grew old for Robin. This year, it was more of a family thing since she had volunteered her son, Blair, to build the sets for the production. Lucky for him that she had, as it brought a wife and two foster daughters into his life.

A wife. Yes, it was true; she'd been at their wedding. Her sister, Phoebe, had voiced misgivings.

"Do you think Blair knows what he's doing?" Phoebe had asked.

"Yes, I think he is well aware, at least on some level," Robin replied.

"What do you mean?"

"I get that they may not look like elated newlyweds right now, but give it time, and they will. They might *think* they're marrying for the sake of the girls, but the feelings are there.

They just need a bit of time to admit them, then this will be a true marriage."

R obin brought her thoughts back to the present. About five minutes of the concert had passed, everything was according to schedule. She had the play almost memorized, having attended so many of the rehearsals.

The narrator continued his spiel, then the chorus chimed in on cue. All good. Simon, a grade 11 student, led with his part, reciting his lines with only a few stumbles. Hopefully, the kid's confidence would build as he got into it.

As the chorus died down, the pianist played the intro to Simon's first solo song. The kid was good, and had grown more so at each practice. The pianist hesitated as she played the first line, and Simon didn't pick up on his cue. Seamlessly switching back to the intro, she played it again, nodding encouragingly to Simon.

The whites of the kid's eyes glowed as the boy desperately scanned the darkness that hid the hundreds of people in the audience in front of him. This was the same young man who would tuck a football under his arm and charge down the field to the cheers of his teammates and spectators, driven and focused, despite the spotlight on him.

But *this* type of spotlight froze him cold. Only his eyes moved, his expression stiff with fright.

Robin grabbed Keith's arm. "Something's wrong," she whispered.

Beth frowned, and glanced at Robin, noticing the way her father turned his hand palm up, and Robin slid her hand into his.

From the orchestra pit, the school counselor, Robin's daughter-in-law, Beth, whispered to the pianist, then motioned to the chorus. The piano played the refrain for the last song the chorus had sung, and the kids gamely went at it again. Maybe this lead-in would thaw Simon's stage fright.

Song over, the chorus settled back into their places, sitting on the floor. Smiling brightly, the pianist again played the intro to Simon's first solo, more loudly this time. Again, he missed his first line. The piano player's smile became fixed as she tried it all once again.

This time, as the last few bars of the intro sounded, Blair strode onstage, and linked arms with Simon, giving the kid a big smile. As the intro faded, Blair took a deep breath, and sang the first line as if this was the plan all along. Turning to Simon as he sang, he squeezed the kid's arm and gave him a huge grin. Come on, kid, you've got this. He squeezed again.

It wasn't until the fourth line that any sound came from Simon's mouth, more a squeak and a whisper at first, then with more confidence, the volume growing, as did the tunefulness. Blair stayed with him for the whole first verse, and as the chorus joined in the refrain, some of the rigidness left the boy's frame, but not enough. Blair unlinked his arm with Simon's, and placed his arm across the boy's shoulders, giving them a squeeze as they started their duet of the second verse. As the chorus again joined in the refrain, he whispered to the boy, "You've got this."

Simon gave a nod.

Blair grinned at him and walked off the stage.

Simon sang the third, then the fourth verse the way he had during rehearsals, belting out the heartfelt tune as if a blip had never occurred.

Robin let out the breath she'd been holding.

Keith squeezed her hand. "I didn't know your boy had a singing part in this thing."

"He doesn't."

.   .   .

The play continued, with only the usual missteps after that.

Robin's foster granddaughter, Friday, aimed the lights at the stage, as the curtain pulled away for the cast's final bow.

When the lights came on, Blair and Beth were center stage, locked in an embrace, oblivious to the rest of the world. The audible intake of dozens of breaths roused Blair from his fixation on only the woman in his arms. "Uh, oh." He lifted his head. "Beth?"

Principal Wayne Tait strode onto the stage, grabbing a microphone. "Ladies and gentleman, may I present Mr. and Mrs. Windstrom, without whom this evening wouldn't have happened."

Beth buried her head in Blair's chest to the tune of the thunderous applause, then the standing ovation from the audience.

"Come on," Robin said, standing and tugging on Keith's hand.

"Where are we going?"

"Backstage to see what's going on."

Becca and Stan, with Randine in between them, pushed by, as eager as Robin to get to Blair and Becca.

"What's the big deal?" muttered Keith.

"The big deal is that Blair and Beth look like they're a real couple now," Robin whispered in his ear.

"But they're married - got hitched a month or so ago."

"Yeah, that was the formality. Looks like this is the real thing. Finally."

Keith shook his head, but allowed Robin to pull him along.

· · ·

S tan and Becca reached the couple first. Stan whacked his cousin on the shoulder, none too gently. "Wasn't that a bit too much PDA for you?" He grinned at Blair, giving Beth a one-armed hug. "Glad to see you guys looking so good together."

Becca might have stood up for Beth at her wedding, but had commented on the aloofness she sensed between Beth and Blair. Now, her friend looked radiant, beaming at them from the shelter of Blair's arm.

Robin pushed the others aside. Resting her hands on her son's shoulders, she stood on tiptoe to give Blair a kiss on his cheek. "I'm so proud of you."

"Mom, it was nothing. I was closest to the kid, so stepped in."

"I didn't know you could sing," added Stan.

"I can't. Didn't you see Simon take over to put the audience out of their misery?"

While the guys ribbed each other, Robin tugged Beth away from Blair's possessive arm. When she had her a little way from the group, she wrapped her daughter-in-law in a hug. "I'm so happy for you," she whispered. "I've seen the way my son looks at you for months, but not until now has he let it out." She drew back to look into Beth's eyes. "You're good for him."

"I love him," Beth admitted.

"I know you do, and I knew you guys would get there. It just took a while, but it will be all right now."

Beth's smile lit the room. "Yes. It...."

She didn't get to finish as Blair's arm came around her waist, pulling her to him. "Shall we collect the girls and get home, wife?"

CHAPTER 3

"Not so fast," said Robin. "This evening isn't over yet. I've got dessert ready at my house. You're all invited, and I won't take no for an answer."

None of her extended family dared disobey.

Leaving wasn't that easy. It seemed like half the town wanted to congratulate Beth on another excellent concert, and to shake Blair's hand.

Especially Simon's parents, who realized just what a giant save Blair had made. Simon's mom kissed his cheek. Pumping their handshake up and down over and over again, Simon's dad said, "Anything I can do for you, ever, just say the word. Anything."

Then there was Blair's other cousin, Greg, with his wife, Aggie, and their two kids. "Didn't know you could croak that well," Greg told him. Then, Greg and Stan's parents, Jim and Phoebe.

All Blair's relatives were there, but for one cousin - Reid.

Reid and his wife, Mona, were conspicuously absent, along with their little son. Usually, the relatives all sat near one another.

"Anyone seen Reid?" Greg asked.

"Maybe they sat near the back door, in case the baby was fussy," guessed Phoebe. Still, it was odd that the couple hadn't sought out the rest of the family once the concert ended.

Friday ran up, hauling her little sister, Randine, by the hand. "That was awesome, Blair. You saved Simon's butt."

"Not really. He had a little stage fright, but would have been fine in another minute."

By now, Robin, Keith, Stan, and Becca joined them.

"Anyone seen Reid and Mona?" Stan asked.

Denials all around.

"She hasn't come around the farm for weeks," said Beth.

"She's supposed to start back to work Monday, but I haven't been able to reach her on her phone," Robin added.

"She probably has it turned off when the baby's sleeping," said Phoebe. "You remember how it was when there's a little one in the house.

Yes, Robin remembered. But she'd also noticed a growing distance with her nephew's wife.

Another day of work at the hardware store. This wasn't entirely what Robin had in mind when she started there. A part-time job suited her sixty-two-year-old self, and that's exactly what Feldman's Hardware required.

But things changed.

After Izzy's death, Keith struggled with keeping up with just looking after himself. Becca had to pull double duty at the store and looking after her dad. Mona, of course, pitched in, although she'd been at the hardware store less than a year. But her pregnancy slowed her down, and she cut back her hours.

Jenny, Mona's little sister, had worked after school, Saturdays and holidays, but now that she'd graduated and had a full-time job as administrative assistant at the high school, she only helped at the store in emergencies.

Of which there seemed many.

Keith had his head back in the game now - different, but managing a year and a half after his wife's sudden death.

Becca divided her time between looking after her alpacas, helping Stan remodel their old farmhouse, and getting the shop underway that took up half of the first floor of that farmhouse. The time she devoted to the hardware store shrank each month. While that store had been her parents' thing, and her grandparents before that, her dreams lay elsewhere.

Robin took up the slack, working full time and often more.

But all that was about to change.

Mona's extended maternity leave was now up, and she was due to return to work at the hardware store the next week.

Except no one had spoken to her.

Not through a lack of trying.

Keith left staff matters up to Robin. Just as well, as people-skills were not his forte.

But where was Mona?

This was ridiculous. What had become of that girl? And Reid - even he had become more remote this last while.

Ever since the teenaged Reid's parents were killed in a car accident, Robin had stepped in to see to her sister's only child. So had Phoebe, Robin's other sister, but Phoebe had sons and now grandchildren needing her attention. Plus, she lived farther away. With only one chick of her own, and living only miles away, Robin spent more time with Reid. Even though he was a young man now, managing the family farm on his own, Robin still kept in close touch.

Both Aunt Robin and Aunt Phoebe had been thrilled when Mona dropped into Reid's life, and even more thrilled at their marriage, then the birth of a little boy.

Mona, although a city gal, fit into their small town and farming community as if born to the life.

Until now.

That first month after the birth of their son was hectic for Mona and Reid. Since Mona's own mother was distant (and, for the most part, uninterested), Robin stepped in. Any new mom needed breaks, a chance to catch a nap, put her feet up, have someone else tend to a disgruntled baby.

Once they got to know each other, and their routine semi worked out, Mona shone. She delighted in bringing young Owen to the hardware store to show him off, and if the baby agreed to the timing, to join friends for lunch at the local diner.

After three months, Mona looked tired. Well, that was to be expected. Reid was back to looking after his cattle on his own, without his cousin's help. Although Mona and Owen had gotten the nursing thing down pat, it still took a toll on a young mother's body.

Did she start to decline invitations out? Yes, maybe, but again, she needed to conserve her energy. Plus, she was building a new family unit.

A few times when Robin had dropped in unannounced, she'd found Mona disheveled, sitting in the dark in tears.

Lack of sleep could do that to a person, and what new mother ever got enough rest? Doing the dishes and tending to the baby while Mona took a leisurely bubble bath was the least Robin could do to help.

Was it enough? Likely not, but every new family needed to find their own way. It just took time.

T his was getting ridiculous. Why wasn't Mona answering her phone?

Reid didn't respond to his Aunt Robin's phone messages or texts either. What was up with that? Not once since he'd become orphaned at age fifteen had he ignored his aunt's messages. Lark and Phil had raised him better than that.

Enough. She needed answers. "Keith," Robin called.

He stuck his head out of the back room of the hardware store. "Yeah? Need something?"

"You'll need to look after the store on your own for a while. I'm going out to Reid and Mona's to see what's up with that girl. She's supposed to start work here on Monday, but none of us have spoken with her."

"If the girl needs a bit more time at home, we're fine without her a while longer."

Robin's fists rested on her hips. "No, Keith, we are not. We're short-handed. I'm only supposed to be working here part time. Becca has her hands full out at the farm. We need Mona to get back here. She's been off for a whole year now."

Keith had known Robin long enough, and lived with women long enough to know when it was wise to keep his mouth shut when he heard that tone.

"I'm taking your truck," Robin informed him. "Don't know how deep the snow is out that way." As she pulled on her coat, she added, "And you could get this floor mopped while I'm gone. Look at the marks the snow and salt have left on the entranceway."

She was doing this out of concern for Mona, Robin told herself. Of course she was. She owed it to her nephew, Reid, and her dead sister's memory to keep an eye on these kids.

But she was doing it for herself, too, she had to admit.

All of her life, she'd played a supporting role. As a child growing up with her parents, their lives revolved around the demands of their farm. It was just the way it was. After making a brief foray on her own in the city after grade 12, she'd returned to Goodrich, settling down with Ron, her high school boyfriend.

Since *he* farmed, she was again in supporting mode, assisting in his goals. Ron had been gone over five years now, but the farm continued, now with their son, Blair, in charge. Farms had a tendency to take over lives - you either loved that or hated it.

Those who hated it, like Reid's uncle's wife Deb, might try, but it was a tough life to stick to when your heart wasn't in it.

Mona, though, hadn't seemed like that. She'd jumped into learning about raising crops and cattle, taking to this way of life. Could she have changed her mind now that she had a child?

Hopefully not. Robin would not wish that type of anguish

on Mona and Reid. She understood all too well what it was like to submerge your own dreams to follow the desires of someone else.

By age 62, it should be her turn, right? Not to sound too selfish, but Robin's existence had been devoted to the wishes of others. Sure, she'd had an okay life, even a happy one much of the time. But shouldn't there be a time when she got to do what *she* wanted?

Things were different now. This **me** generation put themselves first. Work-life balance, and their own needs came first. Not like it had been in Robin's day.

Ron was gone now. Blair had a family of his own and seemed content. It had taken him a while to step out from beneath his father's shadow, but he now ran the agricultural operation the way he saw fit. His life seemed on track with a wonderful wife and two foster daughters.

Seemed a good time for Robin to come into her own.

Initially, working at Keith's hardware store fit that bill. She got out of the house, met people, offered advice, and got to put her management skills to good use. Certainly, Keith lacked in that latter area now that Izzy passed away and no longer worked her behind-the-scenes magic, although he'd deny any such deficit. Their daughter, Becca, could have stepped into that role, but she and Keith butted heads. Badly. Besides, the hardware store was only a duty for Becca, not a passion, the way her alpacas and craft goods store were.

Fulfilling part-time work suited Robin to a tee. Until it didn't. Oh, the work was still okay. In fact great, if only she could go back to part-time hours. She still had volunteer work to do in the community of Goodrich. She had friends to spend time with and needed down-time to pursue her hobbies and whatever took her fancy. This working eight- or ten-hour days, six days a week, was too much for a sixty-year-old soul. She needed Mona back at work.

Surely, everyone could understand that?

Accelerating to power through some drifts, Robin made it to the Manson farmyard in relatively good time, the gravel roads in reasonable winter condition.

That changed when she got to Reid's place. Usually her nephew was scrupulous about keeping his lane and entranceway plowed of snow. If you didn't keep up with it, the stuff accumulated, and drifts hardened until clearing a path took monumental effort.

Eyeing the drifts in front of her, Robin questioned if she could make it through, even with Keith's four-wheel-drive truck. Putting on the flashers, she pulled partway into the yard's approach, as far as she safely could, without risking getting stuck.

Living in town this winter, Robin had gotten out of the habit of always wearing her big winter boots. These ankle-high hikers served well enough on the shoveled walks of the town of Goodrich. She sighed, and got out of the truck, zipping up her coat and leaving the keys in the ignition. If anyone needed to get by, they'd simply move the truck out of the way.

Trudging through the drifts, Robin was happy to see the tractor working in the distance, grinding a bale to feed the cattle. At least Reid was on the job; maybe he'd had breakdowns that prevented him from plowing his lane. He was a good lad.

Trying not to puff, Robin approached the house. Either she was getting old, or out of shape; one of the two she could do something about, and needed to get on it.

Reid, and his parents before him, always kept the steps and their deck that led to the back door snow-free. Not now. There was one narrow path, barely a foot wide. Beside it was tramped down snow, the kind that built up after days or weeks of tromping feet. Robin grimaced. She didn't envy the effort it would take for someone to hack through the frozen ice, sludge, and snow to clear off these steps.

Wasn't this a hazard when carrying a baby? She'd better mention it to Reid.

As was her norm, Robin knocked on the door, stuck her head in to announce herself, then entered the house.

No response.

From another room, she could hear the baby crying, those annoyed shrieks of a child who believed no one had the right to continue to ignore his needs for. No other sound, though.

CHAPTER 5

R emoving her dripping hikers and placing them on the boot tray, Robin again called out. "Hello? Anyone here? It's Robin."

No response.

The entryway led directly to the kitchen, a kitchen almost as familiar to her as her own. Countless hours she'd spend here with her sister, Lark, when their boys had been small. Although when Reid was in charge of the house on his own, the level of tidiness differed from when his mother was alive. With Mona's arrival, the state of the kitchen had stepped up a notch. Or two. Or three.

But not now. Soiled pots filled the sink. Mugs with dredges of coffee in them littered the counters. Dirty dishes stacked haphazardly in the center of the table, with more lining the edges. A bachelor pad gone wrong, very wrong.

Had they been ill, unable to maintain the basics in their house? Shame on these two young people for not calling for assistance when they needed it. She'd give Reid a piece of her mind about that. What was family for, if not to help out?

The baby's shrieks pulled her. No one could resist such an

obvious cry for help. Maybe Mona was in the shower and couldn't hear. Robin listened. No sound of running water.

Sticking her head around the doorway to the living room, Robin peeked in. It took a moment for her eyes to adjust to the dim light. The drapes covering both windows were drawn tightly shut. In the middle of the room, Owen clung to the sides of his playpen, tears and snot streaming down his face, as he bellowed in outrage at his treatment.

"Oh, you poor mite." Robin rushed to lift the child from his confinement. He was only halfway into her arms where her nose caught the reason for his discontent. Remembering all too well how even the best-applied diaper could leak, she held Owen slightly away from her body.

Turning, she started at the sight of Mona sitting silent and unmoving in the chair, not two feet away.

"Mona?" Robin had to repeat the young woman's name twice before there was a reaction. Still no sound, but Mona turned her head in Robin's direction.

Despite the dim lighting, Robin could see that Mona's face was just as wet with tears as was her son's. Mona's hands were the only thing that moved, her fingers shredded a tissue into sodden, tiny pieces.

"Mona, dear? Are you all right? What's wrong?"

Mona raised her eyes to Robin's face. Her lips parted, but no sound emerged.

"Oh, my dear." Owen squirmed, releasing odors that made Robin hold her breath. "Look. I'll go and take care of this little man, then be right back. Don't move." Why did she add that last bit? It didn't look like Mona had moved for quite some time.

The baby's room was in better shape than the kitchen, but not by much. Although the supply of diapers was running precariously low, there were a few left, plus an almost full container of baby wipes. Laying Owen on the change table, and strapping him on, Robin undid the snaps between his legs.

"Holy guacamole!" Keeping one hand on the child's chest, Robin averted her face, pulling her t-shirt up to cover her nose and mouth. Had she forgotten just how truly loathsome some diaper changes could be?

Peeling the tabs off of the diaper released more of the odious stuff stench. Hoisting his lower half by his ankles, she placed a cloth beneath his body to catch any escaping dregs or chunks. "Suck it up," Robin told herself. "Get this job done, then see what's up with this little one's mom."

Clean-up took way more wipes than usual. Really, he needed a bath, but given the state of the rest of the house, she had no idea what condition the bathroom would be in. Once his little bottom was cleaned, Robin got a good look at his skin. Red. Angry-looking. The kind of irritation that could come with too-infrequent diaper changes. Picking him up, she opened the curtains wide to let in the sunlight. The irritation was worse than she'd thought. Cooing to the baby, she searched the change table's compartments until she found some diaper rash ointment and smeared it generously on the child's bottom and groin. Poor wee tyke. No wonder he'd been howling.

What was going on? This was unlike either Mona or Reid, who'd both been thrilled about being parents. "Let's go see your mommy and figure out what's up." Dry and clean, Owen's usually sunny disposition returned. Or maybe it was the attention he enjoyed.

"Mona?" Robin called as they went down the hall. "Here's your boy, all clean and cheery again."

No answer. Mona had not moved, not even to reach for her child.

"Let's let a little sunlight into this room, shall we?" Neither Owen nor Mona replied, although Owen latched onto a lock of Robin's hair, giving a yank, giving his great aunt a toothless, drooly grin.

With the additional light, Robin's heart sank. Soiled cups and dishes littered the end and coffee tables. The room gave off the odor of a place that had not been aired out in a long time.

Then there was Mona. Her usually shiny hair hung lank and greasy, last night's bedhead still in evidence. Stains liberally dotted her sweatshirt; there were more blotches of old food and baby spit-up than clean areas.

Worse was the young woman's face. A countenance devoid of any expression, that is, until you looked into her eyes. There you saw the devastation.

"Mona! Oh my dear, what has happened?"

CHAPTER 6

I gnoring Owen's protests, Robin returned the baby to his playpen. She quickly picked up a squeeze toy, waving it until he reached for it, letting himself plunk onto his bottom while examining his toy.

Robin crouched at the side of Mona's chair, stilling the young woman's restless fingers by covering them with her own and giving a squeeze. "What is it, dear? What's happened?"

Mona shrugged, her gaze fixed on their hands.

"Mona, this isn't like you. What's going on?" She gave the girl's hands a shake.

This time, Mona shrugged.

"Okay, girl. Up with you." Robin pulled on Mona's hands, forcing the young woman to her feet. Since when had Mona become so slight? Sure, breastfeeding took a lot out of a mother, but now there was nothing to her nephew's wife. Damping down her alarm, Robin strove to keep her voice soothing. "I know. It's tough looking after a baby. It can knock the stuffing out of the best of us. Lucky when we were having babies, my sisters and I had each other. I tell you, there were days when we threw all the kids together, hoped for the best, and shared copious cups of tea." Then, she added, "Or wine, on the odd occasion. Sometimes we'd even leave the dads with the kids and take off for a girls' night out."

None of what she said got a rise out of Mona, but she allowed the older woman to guide her down the hall to the bathroom.

Robin flipped on the light and looked in. Phew! At least it wasn't too bad. Debris littered the counter surrounding the sink, but the bathtub looked in not bad shape. It was new. In the latter stages of her pregnancy, Mona had a tough time getting comfortable. Reid installed a new bathtub, a whirlpool one, with jets focusing warm water on Mona's lower back.

Robin lowered Mona to the closed toilet seat. "You sit right there, girl, while I pour you a bath. Nothing more relaxing than that. Have a soak, shampoo your hair, and you'll feel like a new woman." As she spoke, she gave the tub a quick rinse, then put in the plug and started warm water flowing. Opening various bottles that lined the tub's edge near the wall, she sniffed until she found the most pleasing scent. Dumping a generous amount into the stream coming from the faucet, the scent of lavender soon filled the little room, and frothy bubbles appeared.

Still, Mona perched where she'd been placed.

Temping down her worry, Robin spoke as if this was the most normal thing in the world. "Lift up your arms, dear." She had to direct Mona's arms before the young woman complied. Robin peeled the sweatshirt from Mona's body. At least the t-shirt she had on underneath wasn't food-stained, just crumpled, and retaining body odor. Kneeling down, she peeled the socks off of Mona's feet. That seemed to rouse the girl. "Do you need me to help you with the rest?"

Maybe the feel of Robin's hands on her body, or maybe the lavender aroma helped, but Mona seemed to come back to the present. She shook her head, then turned it to look at the half-filled tub.

"Yeah, looks inviting, doesn't it?"

Did Mona's lips turn up ever so slightly at the corners? "Owen," she whispered.

"Don't worry about him. I'll look after the baby while you have yourself a relaxing bath."

As Mona hesitated, Robin said, "Go on. It will do you a world of good. Owen and I will be waiting for you when you're finished. Take your time."

Mona stood, this time the ghost of a smile taking over her features. "Thanks."

Robin left, closing the bathroom door behind her, but not locking it. Something told her she wanted to be able to get back in if Mona needed her. She waited until she heard the faucet turn off, and the tub's jets come on. Good.

Hoping the closed bathroom door and the sound of the jets would cover her words, Robin pulled out her cell phone, dialing her nephew. "Reid, I'm at your house. I need to see you right away."

"Can't, Aunt Robin. I'm doing chores."

"Reid Manson, I don't care. Those blasted cattle can wait. This is your wife and son I'm talking about. If you are not here within 20 minutes, I'm calling your cousins, aunt and uncle to descend here en masse."

Knowing his aunt would make good on her promise, Reid finished shredding the rest of that bale, mixing it with barley, then distributing it to his waiting herd of hungry cattle. That would hold them until he had time to get the bales of hay to them.

Four minutes to spare by his watch. Stomping the snow from his boots, he took a deep breath before opening his back door. Who knew what sight might have met Aunt Robin's eyes when she entered his house? Part of him bristled at his extended family's perceived right to enter his life whenever they chose. But maybe that was all right when he was at a loss as to what to do.

Reid stiffened his shoulders. He'd come a long way from that terrified fifteen-year-old boy, the only survivor of the car accident that took the lives of both of his parents. Yeah, it sucked, and life was unfair. But he'd survived. His dad's brother and his wife had moved into the house with him until Reid finished high school. Aunt Deb was not made for farm life, no matter how much she tried. For his wife's sake, Uncle Don tried, he really did, but it just didn't work. Twice they tried, in between stints in the city. The lure of the urban area finally won out, and Don and Deb moved away, leaving Reid to take over the farm on his own.

That had been all right. After all, he was 20 then, no longer a kid, and he'd grown up working the land and the cattle. When those moments of fear, terror, actually, welled up, he'd had his Uncle Jim and Uncle Ron to lean on. And his cousins. Blair, Stan, and Greg might give him a hard time, but they were always there when he needed them.

Until now.

CHAPTER 7

He couldn't stand outside his own door all day. Aunt Robin would make good on her promise to call in reinforcements.

But still he lingered. The same way he'd lingered every time he opened this door over the last months, never knowing what he'd find.

This was so different from those early days of his marriage when he couldn't wait to see Mona, to share incidents from their days. Sure, she'd had a rough pregnancy, but they'd looked forward to the birth of their child.

Those first few months after Owen's birth were tough; they'd known they would be, as did every new parent. But they loved the little guy. His smiles and his cuddles got them through the sleepless nights and the endless demands of an infant.

When had it changed?

. . .

"There you are."

Aunt Robin stood there with her hands on her hips. Never a good sign.

But there were other positive signs. From the other side of the kitchen island, he heard the swish of water made by the dishwasher. The table was cleared of dishes and wiped clean. He could not recall the last time that table top had been free of debris.

Wait! Oh, no. He hadn't had time to go through the mail for at least a week, maybe more. There were probably bills that needed to be paid. His head swiveled, looking for the haphazard stacks that had littered the table.

"Don't get your knickers in a bunch. All you mail is there, in a pile beside the phone." She nodded toward the now nearly stacked envelopes. "Mind telling me what's going on around here?"

That question was rhetorical, Reid knew. Whether he minded or not, Aunt Robin would have her answers. He only wished he had some to give her.

He noticed that one of the kitchen counters was now free. The stack of dirty pots and pans near the sink had diminished. Aunt Robin wore a pair of yellow rubber gloves.

In the center of the kitchen was Owen's playpen, the child bouncing and gurgling at the sight of his father. "Hey, little man." Reid bent over to hoist his son into the air, blinking his eye as a trail of drool escaped the child's mouth, trickling downward, obeying gravity. This wasn't his first rodeo with a teething child perched above his head. "Are you being a good boy?" He tried glancing around for signs of Mona without Robin noticing. No such luck; he'd learned as a small boy that nothing got past her eye.

"Your wife is having a well-deserved bubble bath."

"Good." What else was there to say? From down the hallway, he registered the sound of the whirlpool tub's jets stopped. That meant Mona had taken a bath, something he'd been trying to get her to do for days, or at least to shower.

"So?"

So. What could he say? "Things have been a little hectic around here." No kidding. "Thanks for tackling these dishes, Aunt Robin. I, ah, things kind of got away on us. You know, with the animals, and this little guy, and everything. We'd have got to them, eventually."

"Uh, huh." Robin's words dripped skepticism.

Hurriedly, Reid went on. "What you've done has given us a great start to getting back on track." Surely that was true. It had to be.

"Reid."

Much as he hated to, he pulled his gaze away from his son and cradled the boy against his shoulder.

"Look at me when I'm talking to you."

"Yes, ma'am."

"When I came here, your wife was in no state to be good to herself or anyone else."

Reid squirmed. "It's hard, harder than we thought it would be, having a baby." He checked to see how this was going over. "It's a lot of work."

"It most certainly is. No one can deny that. That's why you have family, boy, people you can call on. Why did you let Mona get into such a mess?"

Reid winced at those words. Had he? He loved that woman more than life. They'd had a great life together and were thrilled when Owen joined their family. Everything was great, until it wasn't. How to explain that?

Reid pulled his knit cap off, rubbing this hand through his tussled hair. "Aunt Robin, I think we're just tired. Owen's been teething; neither of us has had much sleep.

"Yeah, that happens."

"It's calving time. I've been busy."

Robin glared at him. "You left your young wife to cope on her own?"

"No! I'm here." He couldn't meet his aunt's gaze. "I know, I know. Mona and Owen come first." A slight edge of defiance entered his voice. "How am I supposed to be everywhere at once? Calves come at any hour of the day or night. If I don't check on them, I might lose one, or more, and I can't afford that, especially now that I have a family, and Mona's not working."

"That's what I came here to see about. Mona's supposed to return to work Monday."

Reid blanched.

His face told Robin everything she'd feared. He and Mona had not prepared for her return to the hardware store.

They both heard the sound of the bathroom door opening, then footsteps shuffling down the hall to the master bedroom.

"Ah, I'll just go check on Mona." Reid made his escape.

CHAPTER 8

Reid gave a tentative knock, then opening the door slightly, stuck his head into the bedroom. Since when had he become hesitant to enter his own bedroom? "Hon?"

Mona's wet hair hung in strands down her back, that hair he loved to brush. It soothed them both. When was the last time he'd done that?

Finishing pulling up a pair or leggings, she turned her body in his direction.

His Mona. There were remnants of her there, he had to believe there were. But she didn't smile for him. He chose to think that her expression didn't show indifference.

"Yes?"

Entering the room fully, he jostled Owen in his arms, making the child giggle. "Have a good bath?"

"It was a bath."

Oh, babe. Where were those days when they'd been so easy with each other? Was this his fault, too wrapped up in the farm? Is this what Uncle Don and Aunt Deb went through?

No. It couldn't happen to him and Mona. They were solid. They both loved it here, wanted the same things, wanted a life they built together.

He could not believe that things were slipping through their fingers. Without thinking, he approached his wife as he once would have, enfolding her in his arms, sandwiching a gurgling Owen between them. "Hey." That was the only word that came to him. He relaxed slightly when Mona laid her head on his chest, allowing him to hold her tight. "Babe, it'll be okay. I know it's been tough, but it will get better and we'll be all right." They had to be.

They remained that way for a few minutes, but sounds from the kitchen penetrated Reid's senses. They had to go face Aunt Robin. It'd be hard, but worse if she called in the rest of the family.

Loosening his hold on his wife, Reid took her hand. "Come on, babe. Let's go talk with Aunt Robin."

Mona resisted his pull. "You go. I'll wait here. I ah, I need to dry my hair."

They both knew that was untrue. Most often, she let it dry naturally.

"Aunt Robin means well." And maybe she could help. "We have to see her. Have a coffee with her. I think I smell some brewing."

Mona looked fully at him. "I can't. I just can't."

Setting Owen on the bed, Reid cradled her face in both hands. "Yes, you can. We'll do it together."

"But the house. She saw the mess. What will she think of me?"

"She'll think you're a new mother, coping with a demanding child." Then he grinned. "And you're also burdened with a pesky husband as well. Robin knows me well; she'll sympathize with you." That didn't quite bring the smile he's been hoping for, but at least her lips formed the start of a smirk.

Hoisting Owen onto his shoulders, Reid then put an arm around Mona, guiding her out of the bedroom and down the hallway with him.

"Hi there, Manson family." Robin greeted them as if it was perfectly normal for her to be in their kitchen, washing dishes and making coffee. "Come on, sit. I hope you don't mind that I put the coffee on. I could really use a cup."

Reid set Owen in the highchair that had been pulled up to the table, its tray clean, with Cheerios already set out and waiting for the child's busy fingers, along with a sipping cup of water.

Mona roused herself from the doorway and went to the cupboard to grab three mugs. Thankfully, there were that many clean ones. She poured the coffee, bringing the mugs to where Reid and Robin sat at the table.

"I noticed two new teeth in Owen's mouth that hadn't sprouted the last time I saw him." Robin started what she hoped was a neutral conversation.

When the silence lengthened, Reid nudged Mona's leg with his knee.

Without raising her eyes from her cup, Mona said, "Yes. He's been teething a lot."

That was an understatement.

"I remember that stage well. Rough on the child, but it seemed even rougher on the momma."

"It's been hard," Mona admitted.

"None of us has had much sleep," said Reid.

"He just seems to need me all the time. I can't get anything else done." Mona allowed the corner of her eyes to glance at Robin. "I'm sorry you had to see the house in such a mess. I've just not been able to...." Her voice trailed off, and she shrugged.

Robin covered Mona's hand with one of her own. "You know, when Reid, Blair, Greg and Stan were this age and toddlers, sometimes I thought it was all more than I could cope with. So did Lark." She pointed her chin toward Reid. "You can imagine what this rascal was like at that age. And Stan and Greg." She shook her head at the memories. "Depending on the time of year, and the demands of the farm, we often didn't have as much help from their fathers as we'd have liked. But we had each other. We knew that if one of the sisters called, the others dropped everything and got together. Believe me, even four toddlers at once were easier when there were three moms together."

Owen pounded the tray of his highchair, adding his input to the conversation.

Robin continued. "But you, my dear, you don't have that kind of support."

In defense of her little sister, Mona said, "Jenny tries...."

"I know. Jenny's a lovely girl, and we really appreciate whenever she can help out at the hardware store, but she has her own full-time job now. That first job is a big deal." Robin was making this up as she went along, but thought it sounded all right. "Plus, she's still young. Only 19, isn't she?"

Mona nodded.

"Mona, you're not in this alone. I know that you were the backbone of your family before you moved here. Now, you're part of our family as well. We don't have any one backbone-type; we all lean on each other. Sometimes we're the helper; sometimes we need help. It all works out." She looked at Reid, but he didn't meet her eyes.

Robin shifted so her shoulder turned away from her nephew, her full attention on Mona. "When you need help, dear, it's quite all right to ask for it. It's not only all right, it's expected. It's what we do for each other. And, if you don't feel able to ask," she glared at Reid, "then get this husband of yours to do it for you."

"But…"

"No buts, Mona. We're family."

Head down, Mona's shoulders shook, tears wetting the fists clenched around her mug.

Robin nodded at Reid, then Owen, jerking her head toward the living room.

Reid got the message and left with his son.

Rising, Robin took Reid's chair beside Mona, putting her arm around the young woman's shoulders. "It's okay honey. It will be all right. I know it's hard, but we'll get through this rough patch. Now, have a little cry, then tell me what's going on."

CHAPTER 9

"Where did that woman put the orders? Blast these women, thinking they can come into my store and change everything around." When Izzy had been around, she kept paper copies of their orders attached to a clipboard. It was always kept under the counter. Well, usually. Izzy used to complain that he never put it back in its right spot. That may have been true. Sometimes, but at least he knew where to find it when he needed it.

Becca had started this problem. Sure, their daughter had come back home to help when he broke his hip and couldn't get around well enough to hold up his end with the work in the hardware store. But did she have to revamp their systems?

They'd had things running just fine for years. He hated change.

Izzy had been more open to new things, and was willing to give a computerized system a chance. She'd started to catch on just before she had her heart attack and passed away.

Mona worked for them and had taken to the electronic

inventory system just fine, but then she was young and grew up with gadgets and technology.

Enter Robin. She'd stepped in to help with the void left by Izzy's passing. She didn't take so easily to the electronic system, but kept at it until she could do most of the things she needed to. It galled Keith how someone else his age caught on so much better than did he. Becca said that was because Robin tried. If only Keith would give it a chance, he'd figure it out too, and see how much better it was. Bah.

All it meant now was that Keith had to ask one of them to find things for him. A bother, he knew, but if they didn't like it, they could return to the clipboard system.

But this afternoon? No way. Much as he'd like to get a handle on his ordering, there was no time, not since Robin had taken off. How did she think that was all right? He was the owner, she was an employee. It didn't matter that they'd known each other all their lives, Robin and Ron, and even hung out some with him and Izzy over the years while their spouses had been alive. They were friends.

But did that give Robin the right to *announce* to Keith that she was leaving for the afternoon? It's not like she asked his permission or anything. Plus, she'd taken his truck again without asking. On top of that, she'd ordered him around, telling him to get the floor mopped while she was gone.

And she'd contradicted him. When *he'd* said they'd manage fine if young Mona needed more time at home with her baby, she'd told him in no uncertain terms that was not true. They *did* need Mona.

For years, he and Izzy had managed this hardware store just fine on their own, especially after Becca ran off to seek her fortune on the other side of the ocean.

Why did women always want to change things?

.   .   .

41

The bell over the door tinkled, indicating a customer. It had been a quiet afternoon, thank goodness, since Robin toddled off as if she owned the place, leaving him all by himself to do everything.

"Afternoon, Keith."

"Good day to you, Aggie, and to your young-uns." Ordinarily, Keith got nervous when young children entered his store. They tended to touch things. They didn't stay put. And, too often, their parents ignored them while the kids ran wild, fingering whatever they would in his shop.

But Aggie's kids were different. Well, the older one was, anyway. He was quiet, barely said a word - a trait Keith appreciated. Who wanted their peace disturbed by screeching, snot-nosed kids? Aggie and her husband, Greg, did a decent job of keeping the younger child under control. Alice, or something like that.

Keith stopped short, almost tripping over the little boy who'd plunked himself directly in his path. The kid looked up at him, saying just one word. "Becca?"

It was almost the only thing Keith had ever heard the kid say. For some reason, the boy had taken a real shine to Becca. When his daughter was here, she'd abandon her clerk duties to play on the floor with this child, tearing paper into pieces, then putting the page back together, as if it was a puzzle. Weird, but then his Becca had always stepped to her own drummer, and this boy seemed to get it.

"She's not here, son." In fact, she was here less and less as her own craft shop on her farm took shape.

Even though Keith had more than generously offered to give over part of his hardware shop so that Becca could sell her wares here, she'd refused. Wanted her own place, she said. Wanted it just to be about *her* and what *she* wanted to sell. Kids.

"What can I help you with today, Aggie?"

"I'm picking up the order Greg put in."

"Greg? I haven't talked to him today, not all week, I'm sure."

"Oh, he submitted the order online, did it yesterday."

Just one more reason they needed to abandon this ridiculous technology stuff. In the old days, someone would phone him or Izzy, tell them what they wanted, then they'd put the order together, ready for pickup. Simple. No blasted computers involved.

"If you'd look in your system, I'm sure you'll see it. If it's not put together yet, I'll take the kids to the diner for a snack, then come back for it."

"Ah…" If only it was that simple. Aggie was young. She'd regard him with that look kids gave older people when they realized their elders had not entered the computer age.

He could if he wanted to. He just didn't see the need to it.

But in the meantime, Robin should be back any minute. "Sure, young lady. You take your little ones for a snack and I'll have this put together for you within an hour."

Where were Robin or Becca when he needed them? Or Mona. Maybe Robin was right, and they did need her back at work. She'd fix this.

CHAPTER 10

Reid returned to the kitchen, rocking Owen in his arms. "I think this guy's tired. He's almost ready to nod off." He looked quickly at his wife and aunt. "Okay if I put him in his playpen? I think he'll be out for the next while." He hated to say it, but it had to be done. "I really need to get back to those cattle. I haven't put any of the bales out yet, and I have to clean out the barn."

Was that fear he saw in Mona's eyes? Couldn't be. She was just tired; they both were, and he was reading things that weren't there.

Robin took charge. "You go ahead, Reid. We've got things under control in here." She inflected enough confidence into her voice to carry all of them.

"Good, then. I'm just in the pens if you need me. I have my cell on." He hoped they wouldn't need him. There was stuff he just had to get done. And a guilty part of him wanted to escape the oppressive feel to this house. What kind of husband and father would think that?

. . .

R obin observed the interchange between her nephew and his wife. All marriages went through blips, but this couple was solid, she was sure of it. They were devoted to one another and to their son. So why did something feel so off?

"More coffee, dear?" she asked.

It was as if Mona needed to consider the pros and cons of that question. Finally, she gave a half-smile. "Yes, please."

As Robin went for the pot, Mona half-rose. "Sorry. I should be getting that for you, not you serving me."

"Sit, sit, child. As a mother now, you don't get many opportunities to have someone do something for you. Take advantage of it while you can." She poured, noticing the tears well in the younger woman's eyes. "Have you eaten yet today, child?"

Mona had to think about that.

Robin spoke into the pause. "When you are sleep-deprived, your nights and days can blend into one another until you don't know if you're coming or going. I get it, dear."

She pulled open the fridge. Goodness. When had these young people last stopped at the grocery store? There were two eggs left in a carton. No meat or vegetables to add to a meal, but there was a hunk of cheddar cheese, with only a slight bluish tinge at one end. Nothing she couldn't cut off. "I'll whip you up a cheese omelet in just a jiffy."

Mona just sat there, although she had glanced at the playpen where her son lay snoozing.

Good. The girl's mothering instinct was there. Getting some food into her would help. Who knew when the last time was she had a decent meal?

"Be right back," she told Mona. Almost as familiar with this house as she was with her own, Robin headed to the basement where they kept the freezer. There should be a

45

good selection of beef in there. She could defrost something in the microwave, then put it in the oven to be ready for supper. These kids needed to eat if they were going to keep up their strength. Farm work and parenting demanded energy.

Setting the cheesy omelet on the table in front of Mona, she was pleased when the young woman picked up her fork and began eating. Things were looking up. They'd be okay.

The microwave dinged, to let her know the short ribs were defrosted. Setting them in a deep pan and applying spices, Robin set them in the oven under the broiler to brown them. Slicing spuds, she prepared a dish of scalloped potatoes, then peeled carrots and onions to bake with the ribs. It might not be her best effort, but it would give these kids some nourishment.

She'd see to their groceries tomorrow.

S upper underway, Robin poured herself some more coffee, and joined Mona at the table. "Better?"

Mona nodded. "Thank you. I can't thank you enough for…" she gestured around the room. "For everything." She paused, then said in a low voice, "I don't know what you must think of me, seeing our house in such a mess."

"I'll tell you what I think of you. You're a young mother going through a tough patch. We all hit them, but then we come out of it, as will you." She squeezed Mona's shoulder. "Honey, you're not alone. We've got your back. All you need to do is ask."

"I'm not used to asking for help. I've always been the one doing things for people."

"I know, honey, and I'm sorry you had to shoulder such a weight at a young age, on your own. Not any more. You're part of a family who looks after each other."

"Thank you." Her voice still tremulous, she tried again. "I mean, I really appreciate it. I don't know what's wrong with me. Everything just seemed all too much."

"I get that, honey."

"I love Owen, I really do. But sometimes…."

"We've all felt that way at times. It passes." At least she hoped it would. She couldn't remember getting into quite the state that she'd found Mona in. But it had been over three decades since she'd had a child this age. Maybe she just didn't remember.

What she did remember, though, was the feeling of being housebound, of longing to talk with another adult, to get her mind off the constant demands of a child, if only for a few hours.

"That's what I came out to talk to you about. Are you going stir-crazy cooped up in the house with just Owen?"

That earned her a half-smile. "Sometimes."

"Well, this is coming at the right time, then. Monday is when you're returning to work. We're so looking forward to having you back at the hardware store." She rummaged in her purse. "Want to see the schedule? I've got it in here somewhere. I thought just half-days for the first part of the week - you know, give you and Owen time to get used to being apart, and for him to adjust to a babysitter." Her voice trailed off as she noticed the stricken look on the young woman's face.

Mona lurched to her feet, knocking her chair over backward. It landed with a crash on the floor, startling Owen from his sleep. "I can't." Mona's eyes widened until the whites of her eyes showed. "No, I can't. I just can't," her voice rising with each word. Snatching up Owen from his playpen, Mona ran out of the room.

Seconds later, Robin heard the sound of Mona's bedroom door slam shut.

Well, that went well.

CHAPTER 11

B ack in his tractor, the heavy steel tines projecting out front digging deep into a round bale, Reid worked the levers, lifting the bale off the top of the stack. Spinning the steering wheel, he guided the tractor into the far left corner of the enclosed field, lowering the bale accurately into the metal bale holder. Although tricky until you got the hang of positioning the bale in the ring just right, these things saved money over time.

Cattle were messy creatures, trampling their feed without care or thought, not that anyone who worked cattle believed these creatures were high up on the intellectual ladder. Cows could tromp more into the ground than they consumed. These rings kept the bale in place; the widely spaced rails allowed the cows to reach through the slats to pull off as much hay as they could tug with each mouthful. Sure, they spilled some, but that was how cattle were. The amount of wasted food was far less than without these rings.

They'd only purchased their first one shortly before his parents were killed. At the time, it had seemed a lot of money to spend on something that simply held a bale, when those bales stood upright on their own just fine. As the cows plucked away at the outside of the bale, reducing its diameter, their long necks stretched far enough for them to still reach the dwindling, round hay bale. Calves easily pushed their way between the slats of the ring so they could get up close to their food source, without having to shove their way past the older, much larger cattle who competed for the same food. His dad had had only a few weeks to observe how the cattle handled it. His verdict was it was worth buying one or two more to continue the experiment.

A young Reid remembered the first time he was tasked with dumping a bale into a ring. Imagine placing a two-ton, 11-foot diameter object into a 12-foot wide ring when you could only see part of that ring from your tractor seat 15 feet away. His first try had toppled the ring onto its side, taking all of his and his dad's combined strength to right the thing. While he tried again, his father waited patiently, trying to keep the hungry cattle from swarming the tractor that they knew held supper.

Now, loading a bale ring was second nature. Usually. His game was off today, as he almost tipped the thing over. Geez. Get with the program, man. Didn't he have enough on his plate without messing up this feeding? This was only the first bale, and he needed to bring out at least three more.

A distracted state of mind when operating large equipment led to accidents. He needed to concentrate.

Mona was fine. Owen was fine. Aunt Robin was with them, and she'd make sure they stayed okay. At least while she was there.

Why did his aunt's presence fill him with hope? Since when were he and Mona not enough? A year ago, half a year ago even, despite the struggles of learning to look after a newborn, he'd confidently believed they'd got this. A baby? Nothing they couldn't handle. Couples the world over did it.

50

But apparently not *this* couple. When had things started to go wrong? When had they lost the joy of being new parents? When had the life of the three of them together started to feel like something to be endured, rather than cherished?

Wait, that didn't sound right. Good thing he was alone with his thoughts in this noisy tractor cab. He loved his wife more than life, and would protect her and their son with all he had in him. Yet, these days it seemed like such an effort to put one foot in front of the other, to keep doing the things that life dictated.

He was used to the grueling hours of work livestock demanded. He'd grown up with it, and chosen this way of life. So had Mona - not the growing up part. She was city born and bred, but had come to love the farm. Sometimes it worked that way with newcomers to a rural area, and he thanked the stars above that she had landed in his ditch in a storm, and their connection grew from there.

He remembered their anticipation leading to the birth of their son, those trying last few months of pregnancy where Mona persevered, determined to make it through, until she held her infant in her arms. Despite her discomfort, life was good and about to get even better.

Those first few weeks after Owen was born were a blur. Sleep, something Reid had taken for granted, was in short supply. Neither he nor Mona were nappers, but had to learn to grab those odd snatches of zzz's when the baby slept. At first, they'd used those spells to catch up on outside chores, housecleaning, prepping the next meals, or just relaxing together. Amazing how one human being weighing less than 10 pounds could take over the entire existence of two fully functioning adults. Or previously functioning adults.

But they loved the demanding creature.

During those first few months, Mona's exhaustion didn't

let up. Owen absolutely refused to take a bottle, so all the feedings were up to her. Reid could get up to change the baby's diaper, but he could do little else but watch helplessly as Mona dragged herself out of bed for yet another feeding. Owen thrived on her breast milk, a good thing, but Reid wished he could share more in the work of feeding their child. It'll come, his aunts told him. Once he's eating some solid food, he won't need to nurse as often.

Owen's first birthday was fast approaching, and he'd been eating other foods for months now, still growing and thriving. Nursing comforted him, and was one way to get him to sleep. At least the numerous middle-of-the-night feedings had stopped, allowing Mona the chance of some rest.

Why then did she still look exhausted? Owen was able to amuse himself for periods of time, no longer demanding to be held non-stop. Why, then, was the house in a worse state than it had been during the first months of the baby's life?

Geez. He was not a chauvinist, and didn't believe housework was only a woman's duty. He'd lived alone here for years before meeting Mona, and didn't keep the place half bad, even if his aunts didn't share that belief.

Before Owen's birth, he and Mona tackled things together, both in the house and outside. Mona did more of the cooking and he did most of the cleaning up in the kitchen; things just naturally fell that way since her food tasted way better than his.

The routine varied, depending on the time of year, and farming demands. During cattle birthing season, he was in the house far less, getting up every few hours during the night to check on labor progress. During spells like that, Mona shouldered much of both the cooking and the cleaning.

Until she didn't.

Now, even though he'd gather all the dirty dishes, load the dishwasher, and tidy everything up, the next time he entered the house, soiled dishes were spread throughout the rooms, used pots still on the stove, remnants of food dried on. There were no meals waiting, no enticing smells simmering on the stove.

Fair enough. When Owen was fussy, there was time for nothing else, but tending to him. But what of those days when Reid entered the house to find Owen contentedly amusing himself with some toys in his playpen, and Mona sitting? Just sitting, staring into space? The drapes drawn, she just sat in the dim room, barely stirring when he called her name.

Worse were those days when he found her like that, but her face wet with tears. When he'd ask what was wrong, she'd just shake her head, or when she did speak, it was to say she didn't know.

Well, if she didn't know, how could he have a clue? If he didn't know what was wrong, how could he fix things? She was vehement that she didn't want him to call her sister, her friends, or anyone else to come over. What, then?

CHAPTER 12

Now what, thought Robin. Mona can't come back to work? Why on earth not? Did she feel so bonded to her child that she couldn't bear to leave him, even for a few hours? Hardly.

The way she'd found Mona when she entered the house didn't seem like a highly engaged mother, devoted to her child's every need. How could she have ignored Owen's screams, let alone the stench? And, from the look of that baby's bottom, this was not the first time his diaper change had been long overdue. Poor wee tyke.

While her sympathies went first to the innocent babe, since Mona came into their lives, she'd learned to love her, too, appreciating how Reid flourished with their partnership. That young man had been through a lot, and deserved every happiness possible. Until now, the family all believed that his happiness came with Mona.

Ignoring her child's needs, to say nothing of the house, was so unlike the Mona she knew and learned to care about.

But what did they know of Mona's previous life? Sure, they'd seen Mona's mother and step-father on a few brief occasions, long enough to understand Mona's view that she was better off with only infrequent contact with them. Same with the elder of Mona's two step-sisters. A more selfish piece of work Robin had rarely seen - so different from the sweet, selfless Mona. The younger step-sister, Jenny, was a different matter. Raised in the same household, she didn't hold as pampered a position as did her older sister, Tessa, their dad's princess.

Once Mona made it clear to her mother and step-father that she was not returning home and would no longer support them financially, the guilt started. Oh, they did know how to play that girl, but to Mona's credit, apart from draining her savings and giving them to her mother, Mona had stood firm. After a decade of being the family's meal ticket, she was done.

As it became clear to her parents that this time Mona meant it, Brenda and Samuel Holbrook groomed Sam's younger daughter, Jenny, to take Mona's place. The writing on the wall, and having had a clear image of how Mona's life had been in their household, Jenny rebelled.

Taking matters into her own hands, she'd encouraged Reid as he sought to rescue Mona from her parents' clutches. Then, Mona firmly back in Reid's house, Jenny took a chance and showed up on Reid's doorstep. About to enter grade 12, she'd begged to stay with them, away from her parents, before they could chain her to them, the way they had Mona.

Family mattered. Having lost so much of his own, Reid could not turn the girl away. Mona didn't wish what she'd endured on Jenny, so it became the three of them living on the farm.

Surprisingly, for a city kid, Jenny fit into small town life. Relief at escaping Mona's fate helped, but it was the animals that lured her in. That, and the friendly acceptance she found both at school and in the community.

To help pay for her keep, Jenny worked part time with Mona at the hardware store. While the owner, Keith, was known for his grumpiness, somehow Jenny wormed her way under his skin. She could do no wrong in his eyes. Even her most outrageous comments or suggestions brought a smile to his lips, and acquiescence.

But Jenny graduated and now had a full-time job as an administrative assistant at the very high school she'd attended not long ago. Flush with a new salary, she rented a small house in town. Those first months after Owen's birth, Jenny spent as much time as she could visiting at the farm, giving Mona a chance to sleep, helping with meals, and bonding with her nephew.

Funny, Robin mused. When Jenny filled in at the hardware for a few hours last Saturday, and Robin asked about the baby, Jenny had shrugged. She hadn't seen him or Mona in a while.

At the time, Robin put that down to a young woman busy with her life. Now, she wondered.

Come to think of it, when was the last time she'd heard Becca talk about spending time with Mona and Owen? Or Beth? These young people used to be tight, hanging out at each other's places all the time. But, now?

She pulled out her phone, pulling closed the pocket door that separated the kitchen from the rest of the house. As long as she spoke quietly, and Mona was in the bedroom, she shouldn't be able to overhear.

"Becca? Hi, it's Robin. Got a minute?"

As if. She knew how busy Becca was with between checking in at the hardware store, tending to her alpacas, doing house renovations, and running her new craft shop on the farm. Still, her friends came first.

Robin wasted no time getting to the point. "Have you seen Mona lately?"

"No, it's been a few weeks." Becca thought a moment. "Maybe more. We were supposed to get together at their place a while ago, but Owen was fussy, a teething thing, I think, so they begged off. Stan and I've invited them over a few times over the last month or so, but they said they couldn't come. They didn't show up for supper at Phoebe's last Sunday, either."

Becca picked up on the hesitation. "Robin? Is something wrong?"

"I couldn't raise her by phone or text message. I wanted to talk to her about her return to work next week, run the schedule by her, see how that jived with her babysitter."

"Yeah, the year has sped by. I'm glad she took the extra time. Three months is not much for a maternity leave. But we've sure missed her; the store can really use her help."

"I agree - with all of that. When I couldn't reach her to talk about it, I borrowed your dad's truck and came out here to talk in person."

"Good."

"Not so good. You wouldn't like what I found."

Alarm entered Becca's voice, and guilt for not being as involved in her friend's life as she should have been. "What's wrong?"

"I don't know for sure, but something's off. The house was a mess..."

Becca sighed. "Robin, I know you and Phoebe have certain standards, but some of us are not you guys, and we're a little more lax about housekeeping, especially when we're busy."

"Becca, watch it. This is not about me being critical of Mona and Reid's homemaking habits don't match mine. I am *not* that picky. This went way beyond normal sloth. There was not a clean glass or cup in the cupboards, the same with their plates and cutlery. Almost no food in the refrigerator."

"Owen must be giving them a run for their money. Stan and I will pop over this evening, try to give them a break."

"Couldn't hurt. Bring some groceries with you, as well." How much else to say? This felt like tattling on the Manson couple, but they needed help, whether they asked for it or not. For now, she'd keep to herself the state in which she'd found Owen and Mona. After all, they were both now clean, fed, and safe.

But there was something else, something that affected all of them. "Mona says she's not coming back to work, that she can't."

CHAPTER 13

"What?" Becca almost yelled into the phone. "What do you mean? What does *she* mean?"

"I don't know," Robin answered. "She said that, then ran into her bedroom, shutting the door behind her."

"What does Reid say?"

"I don't know. He's in the tractor; I tried calling him, but he probably couldn't hear his phone ring over the noise of the engine."

"Maybe." Stan always answered her calls or texts when he was in his tractor. But Reid might be using an older machine that didn't have bluetooth. Still, the guy should be on the alert for a call from his wife. What if something happened to the baby, and they needed him? She kept those thoughts to herself. "Reid and Mona are not flush. I understood that Mona's salary was a big help to them, and it was a sacrifice for them to do without it these last 9 months after Mona's maternity leave payments ended."

"I know. Money's not everything, but that extra bit of income can even out the irregularities of a farm's cash flow.

And with cattle prices down, and feed prices up…." Robin let her voice trail off. While she might no longer live on the farm where she'd spent most of her adult life, she kept herself in the loop. Once a farmer, always a farmer. It got into your blood.

It was that way with Reid, Robin knew, and she'd thought Mona had succumbed to the same lure. Had motherhood changed her that much?

B ecca's musings took a turn that did not do her proud. Sure, she loved Mona and Reid, and wanted the best for them. But she wanted the best for herself as well. Was that too much to ask?

Without Mona putting in hours at the hardware store, there was a gap - a huge gap. Keith, her dad, would love for Becca to fill those hours. This was an ongoing feud between them.

Keith inherited the hardware store from his father, and he firmly believed that Feldman's Hardware was an institution that needed to be handed down to the third generation. Her.

But Becca's heart was not in being a town shopkeeper, never had been. That was part of the reason she'd fled after grade 12, seeking solace in the rural areas of Europe. It had taken years, but slowly, ever so slowly, she thought her dad was coming to see that his hardware shop would not be Becca's life. Her alpacas were, and the craft shop where she planned to stock with items made from alpaca fleece, and locally grown and created products.

Now, if Mona didn't return to work, would her dad up the pressure for Becca to work for him? Oh, that was so not going to happen, if she had any say in it. And she would.

But without Mona's help, that left a huge gap at the

hardware store. Keith didn't take to many people, but he liked Mona. They'd never get him to agree to hire someone else. That meant that without Mona, Becca would need to work there.

Shelving those thoughts to a compartment in her head marked Later, Becca resumed her conversation with Robin. "This doesn't make sense. It was always Mona's plan to return to work after her maternity leave. Initially, she was going to take six months home with Owen, then she decided to extend it to a full year. She told me how she and Reid had to work out their finances with care, so they could manage that extra half a year. It'd be tight, but it was what they wanted to do." Now, what was going on?

Becca had another thought. "She hasn't found a different job, has she?" It's not like positions were plentiful in a small town like Goodrich.

"She didn't say. When I mentioned her coming back to work, she just said she can't."

"Is Owen ill? Something wrong with him?"

"Not that I know of. Reid didn't mention anything, and Owen looked fine to me." Other than that diaper rash.

"We need to talk to both Reid and Mona. Are you still at their place?"

"Yes."

"Can you stay there for a while? I can be there in half an hour."

"All right."

"I'll see if Stan can come to take over Reid's chores so we can talk with him. See you in a bit."

R obin remembered something, calling Becca back. "I almost forgot. Don't come with your car. There are drifts on the road, plus Reid's entranceway is blocked in. You might want to come with Stan in his truck."

"Okay, we'll be there."

Robin braced herself for the next call, anticipating push-back.

His cell phone went straight to voicemail. Figures. He rarely had the thing with him, or charged. She dialed the hardware store.

"Feldman's Hardware. Keith Feldman speaking. How may I help you?"

Well-rehearsed words, but Robin knew that underlying, harried tone, the one Keith's voice took on when his frustrations mounted. Well, they were about to get worse.

"Hi, Keith. I need you...."

"No, Robin, I need you. Aggie's here to pick up an order Greg sent in, but I can't find any paperwork about it anywhere. Where did you put it this time?"

"In the same place every order sits - on the computer, under the tab marked Customer Orders."

"You know I don't have time to be mucking around with any computer. Why isn't it written here in plain sight, on ordinary paper?"

"Because that's not the way we do things now. Those scraps of paper got lost all too often. You were always misplacing them."

"But...."

She cut off his words. "Doesn't matter now. We have bigger problems. Tell Aggie we'll run the order out to Greg first thing tomorrow morning."

"Now, who is going to do that? I'm...."

"*You* are. I'll help you get it ready. But right now, I need you out here at Reid and Mona's place."

"Is something wrong with the kids?"

"No. Yes."

"That's clear."

"Mona says she can't come back to work."

"I told you that if the girl needs more time, we'll manage without her."

"No, we won't." She hurried on before he could launch into anything. "Besides, I think she needs the work, needs to get out of the house. Just get out here now. We might need your help to convince Mona."

"Why would I do a thing like that?" There were noises on the other end of the phone. "Becca just dropped in. She says she's on the way out to get Stan, then they're going to Mona and Reid's. You have lots of reinforcements for whatever scheme it is you're hatching. I'm staying here. *Someone* has to work."

"Put Becca on the line." Robin could hear grumbling, but Keith did as she asked. "Becca, please bring your dad with you. We might need Keith to make Mona feel welcome."

"Did I hear you right?" Becca asked. "*My* dad making someone feel welcomed?"

There was a masculine snort in the background.

"Just bring him." Robin didn't have time for Keith's quibbling.

Keith took the receiver from his daughter. "Not everyone is free to run off when they take a fancy. I have a store to run, and since you left, I'm all alone here. What if a customer comes in?"

"You're going to have far more problems than shutting down an hour early if you don't have sufficient staff to run your store. Just get here."

"Robin Norly Windstrom! Since when do you have the right to boss me around?" Keith spoke to dead air. That woman got under his skin.

CHAPTER 14

Owen let out a squeal. Mona was holding him too tightly. With him, it had to be just right - too tight, and he complained, too loose and he squirmed. Some days it was hard to please her child. Nothing seemed good enough; she was not good enough.

Guilt. Again. What mother would feel this way about her son? He was just a baby, had barely been on this earth for a solid year yet. Yet what a demanding year this had been.

Somehow, she'd thought she'd been up for it. And she was to start with. That first month was rough, but she'd reveled in holding this tiny being in her arms, the miracle of creating life, the cuddles, the dependency, the awesome responsibility.

But that initial elation wore off. Maybe adrenalin got parents through those initial stages when their lives were turned upside down by a creature with incessant demands. That energy faded away.

Everyone told her this was normal, as was sleep deprivation for new moms. She got that. She was no different from others in her situation. Yet, why did she feel different? So on her own.

She was not alone. Reid was wonderful juggling his work chores with helping her and Owen. She knew he shouldered the bulk of the responsibilities and did it without complaining. Yet, she caught him watching her sometimes, wondering why she didn't seem to have moved since he left the house hours ago. After he'd fed the cattle, then come in to make breakfast for them, and cleaning up the kitchen, he'd return around noon to find no signs of meal preparations underway.

He still said nothing about it, even when it happened time after time, until it became the norm - their norm. His face got that pinched look, but he didn't complain, just picked up Owen when the baby awoke with a cry, and changed the child's diaper before placing him in Mona's arms.

Her reluctant arms.

She loved her child, she truly did, as she did her husband. Both were the best things that had ever happened to her; she felt that to the depth of her marrow. Yet where had this lethargy come from? Everything, but everything, felt like such an effort.

Never had she felt such push/pull emotions.

Not true. When bearing the financial responsibly for her parents and step-sisters, she'd felt split in two. They needed her, yet why was the burden solely on her shoulders?

She'd walked away from that life. This time, she couldn't.

Could she?

Would they be better off without her?

CHAPTER 15

S tan held the door for Becca, then followed her inside Reid and Mona's place. Stomping the snow off his boots, he went to where Mona sat at the kitchen table, baby Owen on her lap. Giving each of them a kiss on the top of their heads, he asked, "Reid outside?"

Mona nodded.

"I'll go see if I can give him a hand."

Keith took more time coming inside, his reluctance obvious. Leaning against the wall, he toed off his boots and hung his jacket in the back closet. He and Izzy had been regular visitors to this house when Reid's parents were alive.

He gave Mona's shoulder a squeeze. "Hey, girl. How are you doing?"

Mona raised her eyes to Keith's and gave a half-smile.

"You feeling okay, girlie?" Not the most intuitive guy, or so they told her. Even he could see she was not her usual cheery self. Maybe Robin was right, and the girl needed to get out of the house. He knew *he'd* grow stir crazy within the same four walls day after day, without seeing anyone else.

Again, Mona nodded, turning her attention to the child on her lap.

Robin motioned to a chair, and Keith sat. It was okay to acquiesce sometimes; let the women think they held sway at least some of the time - a secret he'd learned early in life.

"Hey, Mona." Becca approached the table. "May I see this little guy?"

Mona held out her son and the gurgling baby readily went into Becca's arms.

Becca danced around the kitchen with him as he chortled. "Wasn't sure if he'd remember me; it's been a while."

Her son was starved for attention, thought Mona. Any adult would be welcome after the neglect he experienced with his mother.

Neglect. Such a nasty word. Yet, isn't that what had happened? Yeah, his basic needs were met. Mostly. With a lot of help from Reid, the kid got fed, and he continued to grow.

But how well? Kids needed more than food and sleep to flourish. They needed love and stimulation and attention. Love, she felt that. But attention? He demanded so much, too much from her, more than she was able to supply. Was it awful for a mother to wish that her kid would leave her alone?

Now, all these people were here, crowding into her space. Robin, Becca, even Keith. Thank goodness Stan left. She loved them all, she really did, by why couldn't they all just leave her alone?

The door opened and Reid came in.

A weight lodged in Mona's stomach, one with buoyancy that rose up her esophagus to lodge in her throat. Heavy. That's what she'd felt for so long now - a heaviness. Everything weighed her down. Everyone.

"Hi, babe." Reid kissed Mona's cheek, then sniffed. "You made coffee. Great. I could really use some."

No one enlightened him as to who made the coffee.

"Something smells great." Reid looked from his wife to his aunt, guessing at which of them put supper on its way. Selfishly, it was one less thing for his to-do-list.

Once everyone settled around the table with mugs of coffee, and Owen happily toddling from one person to the other, Robin started.

Mona tensed. She guessed what was coming next.

One trait Robin shared with her sisters was bluntness. Not all the time, but when called for. "Mona, we're all here as your friends to talk about your return to work."

Her shoulders rigid, Mona looked at no one. She'd already told Robin she couldn't, but had the woman listened? No, instead, she'd called in reinforcements.

Becca weighed in. "We're really looking forward to having you back. The place hasn't been the same without you."

"The customers keep asking when you'll be back," added Robin.

Keith agreed. "I had two people ask yesterday. You've certainly made friends in this town."

Mona's eyes welled with unshed tears. Please, please, don't let them fall. Why couldn't these people just leave her alone? It was harder when they were nice to her. If only they knew what went on in her head, they wouldn't want someone like her around.

"That's great, honey, isn't it? But how could anyone not want her around?" Reid, ever supportive. If he could see inside her mind, he might feel differently. No, that was something she could not risk. Ever. She needed Reid. He was everything, him and Owen. So why wasn't she ecstatically happy? She had it all, didn't she? Get it together,

Mona told herself. Be the person these people want me to be.

Robin cut into Mona's reverie. "What have you lined up for babysitting?"

Babysitting? Mona's eyes flew to Reid's. Had he done something? No, when they'd talked about this months ago, she'd said she'd handle it. Where had the time gone? Looking around the table, she noticed everyone's eyes on her, waiting for her response.

Any decent mother would have thought about this, had it all worked out way ahead of time. That's what mothers did, wasn't it? Good mothers, that is.

"I, ah..." Words wouldn't come. How could she admit to these people - friends and family - that she had made no arrangements, had not given the care of her child one iota of thought? What kind of mother would neglect something so critical?

With one hand grasping the leg of the adult closest to him, Owen pulled himself around until he grinned, drooling up at his mother. Glad of the excuse, Mona reached down. Gathering the child in her arms, she buried her face in his neck. Owen giggled, anticipating the raspberries that usually happened when someone's lips came near that part of his body. Mona did what her son expected, only his giggles didn't bring answering laughter from her. Think, Mona, think.

Surprisingly, it was Keith who came to her rescue. "Babysitter?" He gestured toward mother and son. "It's obvious she does not want to be away from her kid, and why should she be?"

"Keith," warned Robin.

Becca weighed in. "It's been a year. We really need Mona at the store, and I bet she needs to get out of the house." She smiled at her friend. "Right?"

Escaping these four walls and the non-stop demands of a baby appealed. Maybe then she could shake off this lethargy, get back to her old self. Working at the hardware store had made her happy. She helped people, learned new things. Customers seemed to like her. She enjoyed spending time with Becca and Robin. Even Keith. But she was a mother now; that was what had changed everything, started all the problems.

Geez, how could she let such a thought enter her head? Much as she loved Owen, being tied to only an infant day in and day out for a year would tax even the most sane person, wouldn't it? And, she was sane, wasn't she?

The conversation around the table went on without her.

"Don't 'Keith' me." The man scowled at Robin. "I was going to say she doesn't need a babysitter."

"Dad," Becca began.

"Would you women be quiet and let me have my say?" Ignoring them, he turned to Mona. "Becca grew up in that hardware store. I don't see any reason why your child can't do the same."

Becca and Robin stared at him.

"You might not remember your early years, Becca. There was no such thing as childcare back then. People made do. We had that pen set up for you that we moved around the shop as need be. When you got bigger and needed more room, I bought extra panels for it, and made it higher."

Tension flowed off of Mona, enough that even Keith felt it. He turned to her. "Don't worry, young lady. Maybe 'pen' was not the right word. I don't mean to imply that your kid is an animal needing to be penned up."

"Dad!" Becca was used to her father's outrageous speeches, but they were usually directed at her.

"Don't get your knickers in a twist, girl. Mona knows what I mean." He pointed at Owen's playpen. "It's no worse than that thing. In fact, it's bigger, and can be moved to wherever in the store his momma wants. She could remain within his sight at all times, if that's best. I presume there will come a time what that play pen thing won't be enough for him. We can give the kid room to move around, and he won't be bored with people coming in and out all day.

"But Dad, that thing hasn't been used in over 30 years."

"So? I buy quality stuff meant to last. If it was good enough for my daughter, it's good enough for Mona and Reid's son." He crossed his arms. Discussion over.

"Do you even still have it?"

Becca answered Robin's question. "Did you ever know Mom to throw anything out?"

"True. But it must be filthy after being in storage for decades."

"Izzy had cleaners she said sterilized anything. She used to spray down all the surfaces in those years when Becca was chewing on everything in the store." Keith patted Mona's clasped hands. "Don't worry, girlie. We'll have it cleaned and set up for when you come on Monday." That settled, he stood up to leave. "Well, I need to get back to work. Robin, you took my truck. Are you coming back to town with me?"

CHAPTER 16

Keith and Robin rode back to town together in comfortable silence. Much as Robin liked to think she was the organizer, the driving force behind getting things done, she'd underestimated the man beside her.

This afternoon, Keith had come to the rescue. No more 'I can'ts' from Mona, nothing but grateful looks from Reid. They took Mona's agreement for granted when she'd raised no objection to their child care plans.

Who knew that it would be Keith who saved the day? All the arguments Robin had conjured in her mind, all the plans Becca had ready - none of these were needed in light of Keith's simple solution.

Again, who knew? Unlikely to win Mr. Sensitive of the Year Award anytime soon, he'd known just what to say and did it without fuss.

Yeah, the guy could be a grump sometimes. And was definitely a Luddite when it came to technology or change, but he wasn't a bad guy.

Even when they were kids in high school, Izzy had seen right past Keith's grumpy visage, to the real boy inside. Watching, Robin had been surprised that someone who'd known Keith for only such a short time had seen through him. *She* certainly had, but then she and Keith had known each other since kindergarten. Izzy was new to town, and she hadn't really stood a chance, the way Keith doggedly pursued her, making all the other guys back off with just a glance. He'd seen what he wanted and went after it, in his tenacious way.

Although Robin knew Keith's daughter would never admit, Becca showed a lot of her dad's traits. Figuring out what she wanted and going after it. Sticking to her plan through hardships. Being loyal to those important to her.

Robin glanced at Keith out of the corner of her eye as he steered his truck toward town. Despite his gruff exterior, he was a decent man. Izzy had been good for him, softening his rougher edges.

Her death had shaken him, shaken them all, and it had taken Keith months to get his legs back under him. Was the suddenness of her passing what made it so hard? Was that better or worse than watching someone you loved struggle and suffer for months?

That's what had happened with Robin's husband, Ron. His first heart attack a warning sign. A stent and medications were supposed to take care of the problem. They did, temporarily.

It had been so hard to watch a once vital man frustrated by his physical limitations. Farm chores that had taken an hour to complete now stretched to fill the entire morning. Even walking from the house to the barn was no longer something to take for granted. Ron hated that he had to stop several times to catch his breath, when walking used to be effortless. Even with the use of modern machinery, much about farming was still a physical activity, one that required strength and stamina.

It hurt to see Ron losing both of those things. Used to pushing himself to get things done, Ron's old ways now hindered rather than helped him.

Their nephews, Reid, Stan, and Greg, looked after their cattle for them while Ron was in hospital, then still came over as he recuperated at home. But while grateful for their help, Ron had hated to see someone else running his equipment, doing the activities he knew *he* should have been doing himself.

Or his son doing. Ron resented that Blair was off on his own, earning money as a journeyman carpenter so that he could buy into the farm or start one of his own. "This will all be his one day," groused Ron. "Why can't the kid stay home and just work here?"

Robin understood their son's need for independence, to not feel that things had been given to him, or to slide into his father's plans, always the underling. He needed to enter their farm enterprise on an equal footing, contributing not just his labor, but his cash. Had their personalities been different, the two men in her life might have worked together more easily. But they clashed, and none of her peace-keeping efforts succeeded in getting either of them to see the other's point of view. Blair felt his dad was ever critical of him; Ron only wanted his son to do his best.

When Ron's first heart attack struck, he would not allow Robin to call Blair. But their extended family being what it was, the cousins soon told Blair, who took a week off of work to come home. Reassured by his cousins, and with a strong push from Ron, Blair left after that week, making his mom promise to call him if he was needed.

Robin agreed. But she lied. She knew Ron would not want to ask Blair for help. He'd said, "If the boy wants to get away from here, then get away, he should." Ron hated pity, and if Blair reluctantly moved back home to shoulder the work Ron struggled to do, Ron's pride would have made him lash out at their son.

Robin had seen it before - the two men she loved most at odds, both silently simmering. Well, Blair silently; Ron less so. A peace-lover at heart, Robin hated discord. It was easier to convince Ron to take things slower than to risk bringing Blair back to help.

In the end, it didn't matter. Ron did what Ron wanted to do. Making that man slow down just didn't work. Retire? No way. Never a pill-popper, Robin knew the extent of her husband's angina pain when she'd often see Ron surreptitiously reaching in his pocket for a nitro pill. Eventually, he gave in, and wore a nitro patch all the time.

A second coronary incident was inevitable. This next one was minor, resulting in just a brief hospital stay of two days, and Robin had fed the cattle on her own this time, since Ron wanted no one to know he was ill. At least Ron agreed to reduce the size of their cattle herd after that one.

The third one was the last.

There had been a time when Robin had a good sense of how long each task took her husband. Since he'd been forced to slow down, the timing differed now. Still, in the distance, she could hear the tractor, and its tone hadn't changed for some time, as it usually did when driving it and putting it to work on different things.

She tried the cell phone she'd insisted he keep with him now, but there was no answer. Donning her boots and winter coat, Robin had set off to check on things.

The tractor was in the pen, running, a round bale impaled on its tines, but still hoisted high in the air. All around the tractor, cattle milled, hungry, demanding the bale be lowered to the ground so they could eat.

It took a while to walk the quarter mile from the house to the pen where the tractor idled - plenty of time for Ron to have dropped the bale and went for the next one. Seeing no movement from the tractor for long minutes, Robin began to run through the snow, frustrated with how long it was taking her to get there.

As she got close, she could see her husband slumped over the steering wheel? Taking a nap? Not like Ron at all.

Her mind slowed, taking in so many details at once. She was grateful to Blair for removing the ladder that provided access to the tractor's cab, replacing it with what Ron called "old man steps". Yeah, they were easier for an old man, or an older woman, or even Blair. All three of them slipped far less often now that they no longer had to pull themselves up a narrow ladder.

Balancing on the top step, Robin flung open the door to the cab, calling out to Ron.

No response.

She's tugged on his arm. His cap fell off, but his arm hung limp. Aware of the dangers around machinery, Robin checked the gears. Good. Ron had shoved the levers into the park and neutral positions, so the tractor wasn't likely to take off on them. Taking him by the shoulders, Robin pulled Ron into a sitting position. His head sagged to the side. Saying his name over and over, and gently patting his face, the only thing that became clear was that her husband was cold. Although fully dressed in winter gear, and with the heater on full blast in the tractor's cab, his pale face was chilled.

A similar cold filled her heart. "Ron," she'd whispered. Feeling for his neck, her fingers felt nothing around his carotid artery, nothing at all. He was so still. So very still.

Her heart knew, she just knew that this vital man, the one who had waited for her, rescued her and lived with her all these years, was no more. But the pragmatic side of her said,

"You don't know that for sure. What if he's just unconscious? Get help!"

She'd dialed 911, then her sister Phoebe, then stood in the tractor beside the seat, her arms wrapped around her husband.

Distance is a problem in rural areas, and despite best intentions, help could be a long time coming. The nearest city with emergency services was over half an hour away.

Robin roused herself, the breeze on her back registering. She not shut the tractor door behind her. Turning, she yanked the door closed, slightly muffling the sounds of the cows' bellowing protests.

Animals still needed to be fed. Pushing Ron's body firmly into the seat, she found the lever between his legs that allowed her to move the chair into its farthest back position. She was able to squeeze herself between the steering wheel and the seat to reach the levers. Revving the tractor up from its idling settings, she worked the levers until she'd lowered the bale to the ground. There. That would have to hold them for now. Bringing the throttle back down to idle, she returned the gears to their neutral and park settings and made one more phone call. "Blair? I need you to come home."

Then held her husband and waited.

Quiet was good. Keith never understood those people who had to fill every moment of silence with talk. No need for it; made it hard for a body to think.

Izzy had understood that - it was one of the things that had appealed to him right off. Being a new kid in town can't have been easy for her, especially in grade 11, in a small town, where almost every student there had grown up together.

Unlike some of the girls, Izzy didn't flap her lips. She sat back, smiled sweetly, and conversed with anyone who spoke to her. But she was just as content quietly sitting back.

Suited Keith just fine. Being the center of attention never appealed to him, and he didn't understand those who sought the spotlight.

He had friends, yeah, but was never Mr. Popularity. Being part of the "in" crowd, whatever that was, was not his thing. Besides, he didn't have time. There was always work.

The farm kids got it - they all had chores and responsibilities at home that came first. Most of the town kids had much more spare time. Except for Keith; he was expected to help his parents in the hardware store.

A younger Keith's longings gravitated to the farm where his grandparents lived. Other than when his mother took him out there, his visits were far too infrequent for his liking. His dad had nothing against the grandparents, just where they lived. Allergies were the problem; his dad's asthma was much, much worse when he was around either animals, or grain dust. Both of those things were hard to escape on a farm.

As a child, his dad had had frequent hospitalizations due to breathing problems. A sickly boy, his father had never been involved in the farm work. As a teen, when he wanted to earn spending money, he'd taken the only part-time job he found in town - at the hardware store. Part-time turned into full-time during summer holidays, then a career he fell into after finishing high school. When the elderly couple who owned the place wanted to retire, Keith's grandparents co-signed a loan for his dad to buy out the retiring couple.

Changing the name above the door, Feldman's Hardware was born.

There was never a showdown about it, more like quiet, unmovable expectations that, as Keith grew up, he would take over as the manager, then owner of Feldman's Hardware.

Still, something about his grandparent's farm called to Keith. Visiting was a lot of work. It meant a complete change of clothes, putting everything he'd worn on the farm into a sealed plastic bag that went straight into the washing machine when he got home. He'd learned his lesson about not taking this seriously enough after his dad had a life-threatening asthma attack following one of Keith's visits to the farm.

Keith's grandfather passed away first. His grandmother

continued to live on the farm herself, selling off the livestock, renting out the land, and tending to her garden. That lasted one year; the winter was just too hard to manage on her own. She moved into town for the cold, harsh months, but returned to her beloved yard for the summer. Until even that got to be too much.

She passed away not long after Keith's father took his last breaths, his traitorous lungs finally giving up. The farm sat abandoned, the buildings falling into disrepair. At least the land was looked after by the renters.

If Keith had had any notions of one day moving out to the farm, his mother disabused him of them. Convinced that the farm was an evil place, one that ruined her husband's lungs, she vehemently did not want to see her son out there, even though Keith showed no signs of asthma.

Valuing peace and being left alone to do his thing, Keith shelved any such ideas, resigning himself to be a shopkeeper like his father before him. It was an honest living; he made a valuable contribution to the community, filling a need, helping friends and neighbors.

Keith loved learning. If he couldn't *do* some of these things, at least he could learn all he could about them, and share that knowledge with the customers who came to him asking how to do some home-improvement task.

Izzy understood. Being a right-hand woman in a hardware store might not have been a dream she had as a child, but she never complained. She was a good woman, supporting her husband, a true partner.

Izzy. Just thinking about her brought a half-smile to Keith's lips. How lucky he'd been. Of all the guys in high school, she'd picked him. Well, maybe his behind-the-scenes threats to other guys who had ideas about poaching had helped, but still, Izzy had been with him willingly. They slid into marriage as if it was meant to be - little fanfare, just a quiet ceremony after a short engagement. Just the way he liked it.

They'd had a good life together, a real team. Like he'd told Mona, when Becca came along, the baby had spent her early years with her parents in the hardware store, much like he had, himself. Everyone in town knew the child, and Becca was set up to take her place as the third generation of Feldman's Hardware.

If only the blasted girl had complied.

Izzy had stepped in. Usually going along with Keith's ideas, this time she hadn't. "Let the girl go," she'd said. "She's going, anyway. If you make this too rough on her, she'll never come back."

Yet, she had come back. When he'd been laid up with a busted hip that didn't want to heal, Becca had come home when Izzy asked. Not instantly, though; that's what happened when your kid chose to set herself up across the ocean in strange places like Belgium, France and England. And on farms there, no less. Maybe she'd inherited some of the spirit of her great-grandparents, although she'd never met them.

A small part of Keith admired Becca's calling to life on a farm, but the practical side of him knew you had to do your duty, step up to what was expected of you. Sure, Becca'd returned to help with the store while he was laid up, but she made it clear this was just temporary, until he was back on his feet.

Izzy to the rescue, again. Izzy had known just the right bait to tangle to make Becca consider making Goodrich her home. His grandparents' farm.

First, the girl had filled the pasture with not any decent, marketable animals, but alpacas, of all things. How impractical could you get? That girl always had her head in the clouds. Then, she got the idea that she'd turn that old farmhouse into a place to live, plus a store from which she'd sell products made from alpaca fleece.

Taking back some of the formerly rented land had caused a stir with Stan Wells. Stan had used that land to grow feed for his cattle. But that conflict brought the two young people together. After working through their squabbles, they seemed good for each other. Nice to see his girl married and settled. Stan had firm ties to the community; they were not going anywhere.

Plus, Becca now had help. Would she ever have renovated that old farmhouse on her own? Maybe. His girl had spunk and determination. He'd say that for her. But extra hands, plus a partner, never hurt. Stan's cousins and their friends also weighed in and parts of the house were now habitable.

Keith could have helped more, if only they'd asked. He had over forty years of carpentry, plumbing, and wiring knowledge stored under his gray-haired scalp. True, he had not actually *done* some of those things, but he knew the how's and why's, enough to guide customers through their projects.

If Izzy had lived, he was sure she would have schemed ways to get him more actively involved in Becca's build.

But she'd left him - died right in front of him, or almost. Why hadn't Izzy told him she wasn't feeling well? He'd have moved heaven and earth to get her the help she needed. If only he'd known.

He was ashamed of himself, for how he'd acted when he found Izzy collapsed in her chair. He'd wilted into a sobbing mess, while Becca and Stan sprang into action, doing CPR, calling the ambulance, and doing all they could to save his wife. That should have been *his* job. He'd never forgive himself, even though a part of his brain knew that no matter who had performed the life-saving gestures, it would not have been enough to prolong Izzy's life. The ambulance people and the doctors all said so. Sometimes these things just happened.

He looked at the woman now sharing his truck cab with him. Like what had happened to Robin's husband, Ron. Heart took him as well. Like Izzy, too young, too soon.

Yes, Izzy had been quite the gal. As was this woman beside him.

CHAPTER 18

Rousing herself from her half-doze in the passenger seat of Keith's truck, Robin gave a rueful smile. Never one to be a napper, somehow, a brief snooze in the afternoon now appealed on some days.

And why not, if it was what she felt like doing? She was over 60 and had worked hard all of her life; didn't that mean she got to do what she wanted?

Apparently not during the past year. Her days had been filled with working in the hardware store - sometimes six days a week. She *needed* Mona back on the job so she could return to part-time work.

Robin didn't need the job for the income - the farm she shared with Blair supplied enough for her living, but it was nice to make some extra money just for herself. Other than for one brief, partial year when she'd left for the city right after high school, she'd always been supported by someone else. She knew that first her parents, then her husband, Ron, had never thought of it that way. Ron always regarded the farm income as *their* money, and when Blair took over, he felt the same way. Still, something of all her own appealed.

But putting in 40, sometimes even 50, hours a week was *not* what she had bargained on. Mona would be back at work in just three days, and life would get easier then.

And so it should. Let these young people take over more. She had paid her dues, as had Keith, the man sitting beside her.

She knew he'd love it if Becca took more of an interest in running his hardware store. That ship had sailed. If it had ever been on Becca's horizon, it certainly wasn't now, as her interests lay elsewhere. She was a good kid, though, and willingly helped out, while making it clear she could only be there some of the time.

Banding together, the women working in the store had started making changes before Mona went on maternity leave. Little changes, ones they could get past Keith, but Becca, Mona, and Robin made a great team, devising ways to streamline the management of the store, despite Keith's protests.

Mona was sweet, and Keith took a shine to her, tolerating small suggestions, but Mona was not assertive, backing off from conflict. Not Becca. She tackled things head on, often escalating fights with her dad by pushing for change too quickly. That's where Robin came in. Having known Keith almost all of her life, she understood the man, knew when to push, when to let things slide, when to wait and approach it another day.

Yes, she understood this man whose bark was far, far worse than his bite.

K eith parked his truck in the alley behind the hardware store, beside Robin's parked car. "If you give me your keys, I'll get your car warmed up for you," he offered.

One hand in her purse, Robin gave Keith a grin as they both heard the sound of her car starting on its own.

"Why people think they can't walk the few steps outside to crank a key in the ignition of their vehicle is beyond me," Keith groused. As usual. Last Christmas, Becca and Stan gave him a gift certificate to have a remote start installed on his truck. That certificate still sat in the drawer under the store's cash register.

Keith answered Robin's knowing grin with a smile of his own. Couldn't help it. "At least come inside while your car warms up."

"I have a better idea. I have a pot roast in the oven, and Yorkshire pudding is ready to join it. Why don't I take your truck home, then you can come over in a few minutes with my car?"

For just a second, duty warred with pleasure in Keith's heart. There was inventory to put away in the store. There was always something that needed doing.

Robin waited, knowing what would be running through the man's head.

"Sounds like a plan," he said. Having more of Robin's company, along with good food they'd enjoy in the inviting little home she'd created in her rental house, versus heating up a can of something and sitting in front of the television in the little sitting room behind the store? The choice was easy.

Somehow, he felt Izzy nod with satisfaction over his decision.

CHAPTER 19

"Your car's warmed up and running." Reid stomped the snow off of his boots as he came in the door. "Are you sure you wouldn't rather I drive you?"

"No!" Mona hadn't meant that to come out so sharply. "I need to get used to this. The roads are fine and I can handle it." At least I think I can, she told herself.

Why was this so hard? Before Owen's birth, she'd loved her job at the hardware store, loved everything about it. She knew Reid worried about her; who wouldn't when she acted so weird these days?

Throwing him a bone, she offered, "My cell's right here in my pocket, and we'll call you if we need you." There. That should appease him. When did she start thinking of her husband in terms of appeasement?

She'd already changed three times this morning. Once was because Owen spit some of his oatmeal on her, but the other two times were all on her. What in the world did it matter what she wore? Once there, she'd don the usual smock, plus the Feldman's Hardware apron.

Why could this child not sit still in her arms? Why did he

have to squirm so and lean out to his daddy? Oh, well, give him to his father, and let Reid wrestle the wiggling bundle into his snowsuit.

"Whoa, little guy," Reid said, reaching for the toddler. "You believe in making life hard for your momma."

If he only knew. "Here." Mona tossed Reid the snowsuit while she rounded up the child's boots.

She stopped short as she noticed the dirty dishes littering the kitchen table. In the rush of getting ready for work, she'd forgotten all about clearing away the remnants of their breakfast.

Silence fell over the room.

"Don't worry about it, Mona. You've got a lot to do, this being your first day back to work. I'll take care of the kitchen and have a late lunch ready for the two of you when you come back."

Today, she'd work only 9:00 - 1:00, easing gradually into full-time hours. That was four measly hours, yet she knew Reid would spend at least two-and-a-half more times that working on the farm today, aside from cleaning up the kitchen, and making lunch.

How did she deserve such a man?

She didn't, and wasn't that the truth? She lived in fear of when he'd wake up and realize what she already knew.

There had been a time when she'd felt confident, even carefree in their love, exciting about starting a family together. That had been before the reality of motherhood sank in, just how hard it was, and how unfit she was.

Mona pasted on a smile she hoped was just right. Reid's uncertain gaze told her she hadn't nailed it. Again.

"Honey?" he asked. "Are you sure about this? If you really don't want to return to work, we'll figure something out. I only want what's best for you. You know that, right?"

She nodded. In her heart, she did know that and

appreciated this wonderful man. But she felt like a fraud, masquerading at being the kind of wife Reid wanted, needed, and deserved. The strain of pretending felt like a balloon filled almost to the bursting point, ready to either explode in a blast of hot air and tiny fragments, or deflate, flailing erratically in unexpected directions.

"I'm fine," she assured him. "Just nervous, I guess." She nodded toward their son. "And it's harder getting ready on time with this little monster who doesn't know how to read a clock."

"He does have his own agenda." Reid made a face as one of Owen's ragged fingernails scraped his father's cheek, just below his eye. "I have to cut this kid's nails tonight."

A chore neither of them relished. A chore she, as the stay-at-home-parent, should have had under control. Did Reid think her negligent? If he didn't, he should. It was just one more thing, piled on top of all the myriad other things that needed doing each and every single day, things she could not get on top of.

How had this happened? She used to manage working in an office efficiently; her old boss had wanted her back. She'd easily accomplished her job, plus helped others with theirs, then went home to cook supper and clean for her family. Now, she couldn't even manage one house and one baby.

Even when she'd started working at the hardware store, she'd flourished. It was all new to her, but learning was a challenge, and she loved it.

At work, Reid's Aunt Robin mother-henned them all, without demanding anything from Mona other than being herself, and doing her job. Keith, the curmudgeon, became a great boss, and even a father-figure. His daughter, Becca, turned into a dear friend, although one she'd not seen for ages, other than that one time last week.

Why was that? She used to enjoy spending time with

Becca, helping her tend to the alpacas, and doing what she could to assist with Becca and Stan's house renovations. Where had all that enjoyment gone?

Did Owen rob her of that?

Geez. What was she thinking? Blaming her aloneness on a baby who'd never asked to come into this world, who'd not yet had his first birthday. The child did not have the cognitive processes to scheme to separate his mother from her friends.

Yet, that's what had happened, hadn't it?

"Mona?" A pause, then a little louder. "Mona? Should I put him in his car seat?" Reid waited by the door, a squiggly child in his arms.

"Sure, please. That would be great, thanks."

With a hesitant look at her, Reid and Owen left the house.

Mona's shoulders sagged with relief. It felt good to have even a few minutes alone.

Then, guilt infused its way into every pore of her being. How could she feel that way? This was her husband, her child, both of whom she adored, truly. What was wrong with her?

CHAPTER 20

Her knuckles white, Mona told herself to relax her grip on the steering wheel. Sure, the roads were covered with snow, but it was plowed snow, with no drifts, and no traffic coming in either direction for miles. What was the big deal?

She'd been driving for 14 years, the last two years on these rural roads. Her car could probably steer itself to town, especially with the new snow tires Reid insisted she had to have.

Mona clenched and unclenched her hands. Glancing at the speedometer, she saw she was going considerably under the speed limit. What did it matter when there was no one behind her? Checking the car's clock, she realized that she would be none too early for her first day back at work. Could she blame being late on Owen?

She checked the rearview mirror; in the set of mirrors Reid set up, she could see her son examining his hands. Somehow, he'd gotten his mittens off. Again. Reid was not good at securing the mittens so the child couldn't remove them. Then, she felt guilty for being so critical; Reid was a wonderful father and did many things well. Who was she to talk? There were so many aspects of caring for this child where she was deficient.

Should she pull over and replace Owen's hand coverings, or carry on to town, hoping his sensitive baby skin wouldn't freeze? There were so many decisions involved in parenting; it was relentless.

If she stopped, she'd be late for sure. That was so not how she wanted to present herself back at work. They used to find her competent, even good at her job. She needed to do as little as she could to disabuse them of that notion. Or, at least, stave off their realization of her inadequacies for as long as she could.

Mona turned up the heat in the cab a notch, thankful for the heating vents in the back seat.

The back door to the business flew open as soon as Mona pulled into the alley behind the hardware store, the spot where she used to park. Before Mona even had the key out of the ignition, Robin was there, pulling open the back door, reaching in to unbuckle Owen from his car seat.

"There you are, my little precious," Robin cooed to the baby.

Mona's teeth clenched. Did Robin think she was inadequate to even get her own child out of his car seat? Relax, she told herself. Studying Robin's face, she read no censure there as the woman cooed at Owen's goofy grin. The child truly was sweet. Why couldn't she respond to him in the same open way that Robin was?

Maybe that's because Robin didn't have to be with him 24/7, always in demand, always pretending to be the perfect mother she knew she was not, battling imposter syndrome.

Mona forced her lips into the smile she'd practiced in

front of the bathroom mirror. "Thanks for getting him. There seems so much to tote when you have a baby." She filled her arms with a diaper bag, her purse, and a soft-sided cooler with snacks she hoped would keep her son content for the morning.

Keith was there, with his boots and coat on, holding the door for her. He gave Mona's shoulder a squeeze - the Keith equivalent of a hug. "How are you, girl? Welcome back. What can I carry for you?"

"If you wouldn't mind, Owen's bouncy chair is in the back seat. It's good for keeping him occupied. I'll come back for his playpen in just a minute."

"Never you mind. I'll bring both of those things. Go get yourself and your little man comfortable."

Comfortable. Would she ever feel comfortable again? Smarten up, she told herself. These people are trying to help, and you have a job to do.

I nside the hardware store, things had changed. The antique, heavy counter remained the same, far too big to move, but between its far end and the entrance to the back room, shelves were pushed back, and a large open area was now enclosed with a filigreed, wrought iron fence, sturdy, and about two-feet high. The area it encircled was almost as large as Mona's and Reid's living room.

Was this the fence Keith mentioned he'd built for Becca when she was Owen's age? Mona had pictured something similar to a dog pen, not this intricately designed ornamental fence. It must have taken the man weeks to concoct the thing.

She felt both Robin's and Keith's eyes on her.

"Do you think it'll be okay?" Keith asked. "As he grows, there's a one-foot extension I can add to the top if he's a climber." When she didn't say anything, he added, "If you don't like it there, we can move things around to put it where you would like."

Mona struggled to get words past the lump in her throat. She blinked rapidly. It would *so* not do to cry when she'd only been in the building a few minutes. They were being nice to her; everyone was. What would they think if they knew what was really inside of her? Oh, how she did not deserve their kindness.

"It's beautiful, Keith. Thank you so much. It's perfect."

It wasn't often Keith beamed. He tucked his chin to his chest and turned away. "I'll just set up this playpen and chair for you, then I'd better get back to work."

I n between making faces at the baby in her arms, Robin studied Mona, catching the sheen of incipient tears. Hormones. It had been a year since the birth, but still… The body did what it was gong to do.

Setting Owen on the counter, she divested him of his snowsuit and hat. "No mitts, I see."

Mona tensed.

"Blair never would keep his on, either. I used to worry about him freezing his little hands, but it never happened. He used to lose them all the time until I resorted to idiot mittens. Best invention ever."

"I have ones for him that tie on. Reid put them on him, but he mustn't have tied them properly."

"Men. Their rough hands don't work so well on delicate things sometimes." She perched Owen on her hip. "I'll set him in his bouncy chair and we can see how he likes it."

Robin misread Mona's hesitation.

"It's okay, don't worry. Yesterday, after the store closed, Keith mopped the floor where Owen will be. He did it again this morning, using Izzy's special cleaning solution, then rinsing with clear water."

"You've both gone to so much work. I'm overwhelmed."

"Nonsense. We're pleased to have you here, both of you. Owen will be the hit of the town, and as for you, you've been sorely missed and we could really use your help."

Owen banged on the tray of his chair, pushing himself somewhat erratically around his enclosure, unfazed by his new environment.

At least one person in the Manson family was happy.

CHAPTER 21

Adding her jacket and Owen's to the coat hooks in the storage room gave Mona a moment to herself, one she badly needed.

Most of her days were spent on her own, well, with Owen, but he wasn't much of a conversationalist, and slept part of the time. Reid popped in and out of the house all day. She was never sure if his memory was truly that poor that he had to keep coming back to get things, or if he was really that thirsty. There had been a time in their marriage when he had mostly come in just to see her. Now, she suspected it was to check up on her, on her and their son, to make sure they were all right.

Did he not trust her to take care of their child?

Why should he, when *she* didn't believe she was up to the task?

Maybe returning to work was a good thing. Now, Owen would not be reliant on just his mother; other people would be around. If Mona forgot to do things, they'd remind her, wouldn't they? And they could just think she was busy with customers, rather than neglecting her mothering duties.

The bell over the front door to the hardware shop tinkled. Knowing she couldn't hide in here forever, Mona donned her smock and Feldman's Hardware apron. Feeling in the large pocket, she found a sharpened pencil and a pad of paper. Robin. Always thinking ahead. She'd have to remember to thank her.

Voices, then Owen's squeal - his happy one - the kind he gave when he was the center of attention and loving it. He squealed like that, more for other people than for her.

Crouching beside Robin was Celeste from the diner. She turned as Mona entered the main room of the shop. "Mona! So good to see you again." She rushed forward to grasp the young woman's hands. "I hurried the breakfast crowd out of the diner so I could get here before this hardware store gets too packed. *Everyone* will want to see the man of the hour, and his momma." Without waiting for a response from Mona, she turned to do some more oohing and ahhing at the baby.

At least Owen took the attention away from her. Babies were good for something. Smarten up, Mona castigated herself. As her mother used to tell her, "You need an attitude adjustment."

The morning passed swiftly, the store busier than she'd ever seen it. While the cash register didn't exactly ring non-stop, the place was bustling as people stopped in to chat and get a look at one of Goodrich County's newest residents. There was the odd comment about why they hadn't seen the young family around town lately, but Robin shut down such talk quickly, saying how new parents needed their privacy.

Grateful to Robin for running interference, Mona had no idea how she'd have explained her overwhelming need to hide out in her house. With the curtains drawn.

What was up with that? She used to love the way the sunshine streamed in through the picture windows that took up almost two walls of the living room. When had she begun preferring a semi-darkened room?

There was little time to speculate on anything, though, as customer after customer entered the store. No one stayed too long, thank goodness. With repetition, Mona had down pat the remarks people seemed to expect of her. Whenever that helpless feeling threatened to bubble up, Robin was there, suggesting she take Owen into the living quarters in the back of the store to settle him down for a nap.

Settle him down. Yes, but settle *her* down, as well.

Living like a hermit these past months had not prepared her for this influx of people.

N oon. With a start, Mona realized the time as Robin put on her coat. No! Robin was leaving for her lunch break, leaving Mona in charge on her own. Keith was out on a delivery, Owen taking a nap. If anyone came into the store, without Owen as a distraction, she'd have to talk to them on her own. Maybe she should try to wake up her son. No, roused before he was ready, he was a bear. Just what she didn't need would be for the townspeople to see what an inadequate mother she was, unable to get her baby to stop crying.

"You'll be okay on your own, dear." A statement or a question? Robin never would have asked such a thing when Mona had worked here before. "I get that this morning might have been a bit overwhelming for you."

That lump in Mona's throat was back, with waterworks rising behind her eyes. "I'm fine, thanks, Robin. Go ahead and enjoy your lunch."

"If you're sure…."

Mona reached for the duster from beneath the counter. "It's quiet right now. I'll just tidy up a bit in here." The lingering gaze Robin gave told her she hadn't been as convincing as she'd hoped.

Robin quickly drove to the little house she rented in town. Once inside, she pulled out her cell phone. "Beth, it's Robin. Do you have a few minutes to talk?"

"Sure. I'm on my lunch break, sitting at my desk. I'll go close my door so no one interrupts us." She was back in seconds. "What's up?"

"Have you talked to Mona in a while?"

"No. We haven't gotten together in quite some time. Why?"

"I'm not sure. Maybe it's nothing. This being her first day back at work, I'm sure it's tiring."

"I can hear a 'but' in your voice."

"Something seems off about her. I can't put my finger on it."

"First day at work. Half the town dropping in to see her child. Worried he might act up, could be lots of things going on."

"True. Yeah, all of that. Still, she's not quite the same Mona."

"She'd had a baby, a major disruption to their lives and to her body. Life will never again be the same for them."

Robin debated. So far, she'd told no one of the state she'd found Owen and Mona in a week ago. Was that keeping a trust or was her omission doing more harm than good?

"Would you see if you could drop in on her this weekend? Maybe have a chat, just the two of you? This might all be the worries of an old lady, but I'd like to see if you pick up on anything wrong."

CHAPTER 22

R obin stretched in luxuriously. Lovely to have a slow start to her day. Mona had started work at 9 that morning, leaving Robin free until she took over at noon, giving Mona a break. Then, while Keith delivered orders, the two women, plus Owen, would work together the rest of the afternoon.

This semi-retirement was more like it - still feeling useful, and involved, but at a leisurely pace. With more time to herself, she enjoyed working her way through the first season of Downton Abbey, while her hands busied themselves knitting.

Although Becca had been hopeful her on-farm shop selling alpaca products would take off, so far it was more popular than any of them had imagined. So much so that she was running low on products.

That's where Robin came in. Socks. Alpaca socks were hot items in Becca's store, with mittens for a close second. Thankfully, neither took that long to knit, so Robin spent some of her spare time creating hand-knit items for Becca's store.

She'd always loved knitting. The repetitive motions soothed her soul and made her feel she was doing something productive, rather than just vegging out in front of the television.

Working with alpaca wool took a little getting used to. It was slipperier by far than synthetic yarn, and more so than sheep's wool. The loops tended to slide off of regular light, plastic needles, but wood, or bamboo ones made it easier.

Keith had surprised her at Christmas with the most thoughtful gift. They hadn't thought he paid any attention when she and Becca discussed the challenges of knitting with alpaca fiber, or the difficulty in finding appropriate wooden or bamboo needles locally.

In a cramped storage area at the back of his store's storage area, Keith had long ago carved out a place he called his own, and woe betide anyone who stored cases anywhere near his private spot. Among his prized tools, there was a tiny lathe. Yes, he would have preferred a larger one, but made do with what was possible. He created wooden pen holders on that lathe, things of beauty from exotic woods, polished to the perfect sheen.

With time and ingenuity, Keith reconfigured that lathe to design a set of wooden knitting needles for Robin - some short, at six inches for knitting socks using a trio of needles, some 9-inch, and 12-inch needles, pairs in the varying sizes. Using his bench saw, clamps, and router, he then designed a wooden box to hold all of these wooden needles, each spot with an engraved label stating the needle size.

Robin could not imagine the hours it must have taken the man to design and create such a gift.

. . .

B ut Blair could. As a carpenter, he knew what went into such craft.

As Robin, Keith, Stan and Becca had joined them at Blair and Beth's house for gift openings December 25th, Blair wondered just what would drive a man to devote that many hours to a gift. While the women oohed and ahhed over the present, no one else questioned the time and devotion behind it.

Stan wasn't a wood-working guy. He could swing a hammer just fine, but his expertise lay more in the area of TIG and MIG welding. Besides, subtleties went over the guy's head. Fair enough. This wasn't *his* mother. Everyone else, including Beth, seemed to see nothing inappropriate about Keith's gift to Robin.

But it stuck in Blair's craw. What did it mean? Did the guy just have too much time on his hands? Did he create the needles so that Robin could help his daughter Becca, get more alpaca knitting done? He mulled it over at odd times over the following weeks.

N ow Blair needed to ask his mother a favor.

Robin set aside her knitting as her cell phone rang. "Hello."

"Hi, Mom. How are things going?"

"Just fine, son. And with you and Beth and the girls? I haven't seen them for a few days."

"That's what I'm calling about. I need your help with them tomorrow, if you wouldn't mind."

"What is it?"

"You know how the door to this house sticks sometimes in the winter? Well, it's doing it now. Normally, it's not a problem, as Beth can give it a good kick to get it open. Or, if she's not with them, the girls come get me.

"But tomorrow we have a problem. I'll be away all afternoon taking some cattle to auction. Beth has a staff meeting after school that won't be over until nearly 5:00. It's cold out, and I don't want the girls to come home on the bus and be unable to get into the house. Any chance they could come to your place after school until Beth or I can pick them up?"

"Of course, dear. You know Randine and Friday are welcome anytime. I enjoy having them around." She thought about the schedule they'd set up at the hardware store. "Tomorrow is perfect. I'm opening the store in the morning, then I'll be off at one when Mona comes in. I'll have some cookies baked for the girls."

"Thanks, Mom. They'll love that. Beth or I will be there to get them as soon as we can."

"No problem, they are always welcome. In fact, maybe they could spend an overnight with me again some weekend; we have not done that in a while. Give you and Beth some time to yourselves."

"Sounds great. I'll talk it over with Beth about a sleepover and let you know."

The next evening, Blair and Beth shut down the lights in the house, preparing for bed.

"The girls really enjoyed spending time with your mom this afternoon," Beth said. "She's so good with them. Neither girl can remember ever meeting their own grandmothers."

"They weren't missing much if their grandparents were anything like those two sorry excuses for humans who supposedly parented Friday and Randine."

"True. The girls seem taken with Keith, as well."

"Keith? When did they see him?"

"He arrived at your mom's place a little before I did. He was sitting at the table with the kids, playing Go Fish when I got there."

"Where was Mom?"

"Bustling around the kitchen, as usual."

"She said she was going to make cookies for the girls."

"Oh, she did, and half of them were already eaten. Robin was putting the finishing touches on a lasagna she was about to pop into the oven. It smelled great."

"Lasagna? Did she think Friday and Randine were staying for supper?"

"Don't think so, although she did offer. It was tempting, but I knew you were bringing home Chinese food, so we resisted temptation."

"Do you think my mother was deliberately making supper for herself and Keith?"

"Looked that way. Why?"

∽

Later that evening, Robin and Keith relaxed on her couch, each with a glass of port and a cribbage game between them.

"I'd say that went pretty well, wouldn't you?" Keith asked.

"You mean supper?" She'd roasted a couple of Cornish hens.

"Yeah, the meal was great, but I meant Mona's first day back at work."

Robin regarded the man. Had he even been there that morning? Had he not seen the nerves all but jumping out of Mona's skin, the sheen of tears so often in her eyes, the number of times she hid in the storage room on some pretext of another. "What do you mean, well? That girl was a nervous wreck!"

"It was her first day and all that. Give her a break. She did fine."

What planet was this guy from? Becca always complained that her dad was clueless, but this bad? "Keith, that girl is not herself. Something's wrong."

"What's wrong is she's a new mother, and that takes some getting used to. Cut her some slack. Izzy was like a whirlwind when we first had Becca. And emotional - I hardly knew my wife. I tell you, she'd either cry, or turn on me quick as a dime. I learned to just keep out of the way."

"And do you think that helped her?"

"Seemed to work for me."

Robin counted to ten. How Keith and Izzy had handled their marriage was not her business.

She remembered times when Ron had either hovered or hid when Blair was first born. Different times. But she knew that Reid was a hands-on dad, and good around the house.

"I think something's wrong with Mona, and I asked Beth to go see her."

"Oh, me, Robin. What did you have to muck into their business for?"

CHAPTER 23

"Are you sure you don't want us to go with you? The girls would love a chance to fuss over Owen, and Reid and I can hang out." It was Saturday afternoon, and Blair had a few hours of downtime.

"No, not this time," said Beth. "I feel the need for some girl time with just Mona and me."

Blair frowned, not sure he'd ever heard the words 'girl time' come out of Beth's mouth before. Usually they visited his cousins as a couple, or a group of them hung out. "Okay, if you're sure. The girls and I will have supper ready when you get back."

~

Reid was plowing snow in the lane when Beth drove up in Blair's truck. She waited until he finished clearing the area in front of the house, then followed the tractor to where Mona's car was already parked.

She could tell by the sound of the engine that Reid had

throttled it down to idle, then opened the cab door, and climbed out. Was his smile not as welcoming as usual?

"Afternoon, Reid. Is Mona in the house?"

Reid hesitated. Yes, she was, but would she want visitors? He tried to remember what shape the house was in, although the days blurred together. Their once tidy home now bordered on something that would make his mother shudder in her grave. "Hi, Beth." He gave her a one-armed hug. "Yeah, she's inside, but I don't know if she's napping or not." She did that - a lot.

"Okay. I'll tiptoe in and leave if she's asleep."

"Ah…" What was there to say?

"Yes?" Beth waited.

"Um, Owen's been a bit on the cranky side lately. We kind of let everything else go while we tried to survive." Reid cast a quick glance toward the kitchen window, but the curtains were drawn. "You might find things in a bit of a mess."

"No problem. We have *two* kids now, remember? Even though they're not babies, they leave a lot of stuff around. With both of us working, well, let's say the house rarely looks like the way Robin used to keep it."

Reid's answering grin was weak, nothing like the warm, open smile she'd become used to since he and Mona got together.

R emoving her boots as quietly as possible, Beth hung her coat on a hook, stepping into the kitchen. No movement, no sound. What was that smell?

Not dank, not musty. Old cooking odors mixed with what? Remnants of meals? Certainly not usual for Mona and Reid's house. In the center of the kitchen table dishes piled precariously, and around the edges, evidence of toast and breakfast eggs streaked other soiled plates. She shoved some back to make a small spot in one corner to set down the bag she'd brought.

Poor Reid and Mona. Owen must be giving them a run for their money. They had to be exhausted. If Mona was asleep, the least Beth could do was clean up the kitchen for them.

Her sock feet made little noise as she tiptoed to the entrance to the living room. Through the side mesh of his playpen, Beth could see Owen spread-eagled on his back, face relaxed in sleep, drool seeping from the corner of his mouth. Only on a baby could that be cute. On the couch, Mona lay on her side, hand fisted under her cheek, eyes closed. Considering the bright, wintery sun outside, the lighting in here was dim; maybe Owen slept better that way. Both he and Mona likely needed this rest.

Retreating, Beth eased shut the pocket door that separated the living room from the kitchen. Hopefully, it would deaden the sounds she'd make as she cleaned the kitchen.

First, she filled the coffee maker with fresh water and grounds. Reid lived on coffee, she knew, and he'd likely be in soon. Opening her bag, she removed the jar of fresh cream she'd brought with her. Reid and Mona loved the stuff, but didn't have any dairy cows of their own. Blair did - just one, Clarabelle, Robin's beloved Jersey. Although Blair was gradually divesting himself of the cattle herd he'd kept, mainly because that was what his father had always done, the farm just wouldn't be the same without Clarabelle. Plus, once you'd had fresh cream, the store-bought stuff would never do.

Friday proved to be a true help with Clarabelle, taking over the majority of her care, even doing the milking whenever weekends or school holidays permitted. Friday and Randine became adept at using the cream separator, although the intricate cleaning of the machine's working parts fell mostly to Beth and Blair. No matter - it was worth it to have fresh butter and cream. Beth would never have believed that one cow could produce so much milk, but once it was shared out between them and Robin, Becca and Stan, Reid and Mona, and sometimes Blair's Aunt Phoebe's family, they made good use of all that Clarabelle offered. Was it economical? Debatable, but this was one of the perks of living on a farm.

Coffee started, cream in the fridge, the cheese scones she'd made that morning warming in the oven, Beth checked to see if there was anything out for supper. Nada.

Knowing where things were in this house, she went to check the basement freezer. One thing these cattle-ranching cousins always had was ample beef in their deep freezes. Rummaging, she brought up a package of ribs, and set the microwave to quickly defrost. Once she could cut them apart, some oil, a nice rub, and some baked potatoes would be the start of a meal for her friends.

Next, she tackled the kitchen. Thankfully, the dishwasher was empty, so after scraping and briefly soaking the soiled plates and cutlery, she loaded the machine and got it going. Next, she attacked the cooking pots sprawling across the counter and stovetop. Looked like things had been hairy around here for days. Poor Mona.

She thought about Blair's offer to accompany her with the girls. If Friday and Randine had been here, they could have gotten this kitchen in shape quicker. But no, that wouldn't have worked. Try as they might, those two just did not have a quiet bone in either of their bodies.

Oh, they did at first. When they'd initially come to live with her and Blair, Randine especially was a shadow of her current self. Friday, five years older, was used to playing the mothering role to her little sister, stepping in front of her, shielding her from whatever might come at them. But Friday already trusted Beth and Blair from her contact with them at school - so much so that when she felt they were in serious trouble, it was Blair she called to come rescue them.

Now, in their home in permanent foster care, the girls were free of their abusive parents, and gradually blossomed under the guardianship of Beth and Blair. It was lovely to see their true personalities shine forth as they grew in confidence and the shadows left their eyes.

What was that? Beth's hands froze in the soapy dishwater. Was she making too much noise and had woken the slumbering pair in the living room? After pausing for a few moments, she heard nothing more, returning to her tasks.

CHAPTER 24

Mona feigned sleep, as she usually did when she heard someone enter the house. It was easier that way, easier than meeting the question in Reid's eyes, his concern, the worry she was powerless to explain away.

Oh, how she hated being the source of his unhappiness, this man who had shown her nothing but kindness and love. And, for a while, a long while even, it had been enough. She'd thought her life pretty much perfect with the man of her dreams and their child on the way.

Then, it wasn't.

Those first months after Owen's birth were tough. That was normal for all parents though, the fatigue, the always being on call, but she knew they'd figure it out. Together.

And they had. Things had improved, and by the third month, they'd developed a sort of routine, or as much of one as their little monkey allowed. Sure, things were messy and chaotic, but when Owen bestowed one of his gummy smiles on them, her heart melted.

Reid helped as much as he could in between farm work,

and Owen couldn't ask for a better dad, and she a better partner.

But the same could not be said for Reid of her. Maybe in the beginning, yes. He'd seemed happy with her and with their son. Then she noticed the shadows in his eyes, the way he watched her, but without some of the joy they'd once shared.

She tried, she really did, over the next months to be cheery, to be all that she knew Reid and Owen deserved. Her efforts at being bubbly left Reid studying her.

Reading had always been her refuge, and she'd searched the internet for delicious homemade meals. The problem was, elaborate, multi-step recipes that looked glorious online required time and concentrations Mona just didn't have.

She'd start in as soon as Owen fell asleep, determined to make that night's supper the best ever. But Owen's naps were unpredictable; she might have two hours, or twenty minutes. It was hard to concoct the perfect Hollandaise sauce from scratch when your kid woke up screaming just as you were carefully streaming the oil into the blender.

Too many times Reid had walked into the house, only giving her a glance as she worked at the stove, striding straight into the other room to rescue a wailing, snotty baby from his crib. With a nod at the kitchen counter, he'd ask, "Is *that* more important than our son?"

No! No, of course it wasn't, but she was trying to do something nice for them, something that would make her feel good about herself.

In the end, she gave up.

W aking Owen was not in the cards. Rolling onto her back as silently as she could, Mona listened to the sounds coming from the kitchen.

That was not Reid. Even when he thought he was being quiet, his heavy footsteps stomped wherever he went. No, these were softer footfalls. A woman. Oh, please don't let it be Robin again. She could not stand it if Robin caught her in such a mess twice in as many weeks.

M ona heard the back door open and the pocket door swayed slightly on its runner as the wind from the outside rushed in. Heavy boots stamped on the mat, and then those boots thudded to the floor.

Reid. In to check on her, as usual. Straining, she could hear voices, but their words were unclear. From the timbre of the higher one, she recognized Beth. Beth, not Robin. At least Beth was kind and uncritical. She grimaced. Since when was Robin not kind, or any of their friends for that matter? They were all sweet and welcoming and helpful. It's just that she shouldn't need their help, should she? She wanted the respect of these people not to be pitied.

She'd been inside her own head so much that she did not hear the pocket door slide open until her eyes met Reid's.

Her husband's head poked back into the kitchen. "Yep, she's awake now, and yes, I'm sure she'd love some coffee." He came back into the living room, only giving a passing glance at their sleeping son. Sitting on the edge of the couch, he brushed Mona's hair from her forehead, giving her a kiss. "Hi, honey. Have a good nap?"

Mona forced her eyes to meet his and gave a smile. "Yes, thanks." She hated that she now analyzed every look Reid gave her when things used to be so easy between them. Lifting her head, pretending to check on Owen, she said, "Is that Beth's voice I hear?"

"Yeah. She brought us some fresh cream."

"Yummy." It was the right thing to say.

"Come on." Reid put his arm under her shoulders. "Let's go try some out in the coffee Beth put on."

Letting him half-lift her off of the couch, Mona tried to finger-comb her hair as Reid led her into the other room. When had she last brushed it, or even washed it? Too late now to do anything but brazen it out.

Beth met her with a smile and a partial hug.

To Mona, the smile seemed genuine.

Reid led her to the table, and Beth set a steaming mug in front of her.

The table. Had it looked like this a few hours ago? She couldn't remember; the days blurred into one another. Some days were better than others as far as keeping up with housework, but somehow, she feared this had not been one of them.

The table was clean now, the wood gleaming in the sunlight coming in the window. With the curtains pulled back, the room was bright.

"Thanks," Mona said, truly grateful. "Coffee just isn't the same without Clarabelle's cream."

"I think I'd better take mine in a to-go mug," said Reid. "I've got to plow my way out to the pasture before I can feed those animals tonight." He kissed the top of his wife's head, gave another quick look at his still-sleeping son, and put on his outdoor clothes. "I'll leave you ladies to it."

CHAPTER 25

I t still bugged Blair. That Christmas gift Keith made for his mother was way over the top - not something casual acquaintances, or employer/employees, would do. Then Beth said Keith was at Robin's for supper when she picked up the girls. Somehow, Blair had the feeling that might not have been the first time. And the way that man had casually put his arm around the back of his mother's chair during Christmas dinner - right in her own house, in front of her family.

What did that guy think he was doing?

Randine brought out the Monopoly board. Sure, why not? Playing with the girls would take his mind off worrying about his mother. Yeah, she was an adult, and not in her dotage, but who did she have to look out for her if not him?

She had to be naïve since she'd lived her whole life here, and only been with one man, Ron. He grimaced. Not exactly only one man - there had briefly been one other, the guy who'd fathered *him* then run off, leaving Robin pregnant and alone. Ron had stepped in, having always had a thing for Robin, and raised him as his own.

Sort of. If you could call that raising a child. From Blair's point of view, Ron had been an exacting taskmaster, critical, never recognizing when the young Blair did anything right. Years later, Robin explained that was Ron's way of ensuring Blair did not turn out to be the kind of irresponsible man his birth father had been. He saw the point, but surely there had been other ways to achieve that goal.

He would certainly never treat Friday and Randine that way. He smiled to himself. Nor would Beth let him.

"It's your turn," Randine reminded him. "You're going to pay me big money when you land on this row."

She was right. He had to borrow from the bank to cover the rent. "While you girls work that out for me, I'll be right back. Need to make a call."

No point in stewing about things, Beth always said. Ask. Find out, rather than imagining. Blair dialed his mother's landline.

A male voice answered. "Robin Windstrom's residence. May I take a message?"

Blair paused. "Who is this?"

"Keith Feldman."

"Where's my mother?"

"Oh, hello, Blair. She ran out to the store, something about an item she ran out of that she wants to use in making supper. She'll be back any minute."

"What are *you* doing in her house?"

Should she just come out with it? Ask Beth what the kitchen had been like when she walked in?

Would Beth lie and say it was fine, or would she admit she'd cleaned up?

Neither woman was in the habit of lying to the other;

none of their friends were. But if she asked, did Mona want to hear the truth?

Beth's eyes regarded her over the rim of her mug - non-intrusive eyes, ones that seemed to say whatever it is it's okay, and I'm your friend.

Could eyes send messages?

Apparently. Because as Beth watched her, the other woman's eyes changed from warm to concerned. Beth reached over and squeezed Mona's hand. "What? What is it?"

That's all it took.

The dam broke and the tears, the ones she'd tried so hard to only shed in private, overflowed. "I can't do it anymore." Oh, how shameful was that, not just the words, but they came out as more a wail than a confession, a wail of Owen proportions?

Beth gathered up some napkins and pressed them into Mona's hand. Then she waited.

While the tears still ran freely, at least that awful lump in her throat had moved on, allowing her to speak. Good or bad, it was coming out.

"I'm done. I can't keep pretending any longer. I just can't do it."

"It?"

"Living a lie. Making believe that I can do it all. Be the perfect mother, the perfect wife. Although Reid can tell you how badly I've flubbed the latter." She gave a snort that came out mixed with a sniff.

Both women gave a laugh.

"Perfect?"

"You know, do it all."

"All?"

Mona mock-scowled. "Can you only speak in one-word sentences?"

"Yep." Beth grinned. "Tell me what's going on."

"I'm tired, just so tired."

Beth started to get it. "You think more so than any new mother?"

"I've seen other mothers. Yeah, they can be tired, but not impossible to get out of bed weary. That first while after Owen was born, and we were up most nights with him, I was tired, but nothing like this. Back then, I'd give anything for a nap, but now naps don't do any good. I wake up feeling just like I did before."

"How long has this been going on?"

"For months, although it feels like forever. I fear I'll never feel okay again."

"Is it just the tiredness?"

"No, it's everything." She mopped her face. "I just feel like giving up, like nothing I do is ever good enough, nor will it ever be."

"Owen seems to be growing and thriving."

"That's a fluke, or it's Reid's doing. He's really picking up the slack created by me. He's trying, but he expected this parenting thing to be a two-way street between us."

"Has he been to the Well-Baby Clinics? What does the nurse say?"

"Of course I've been taking him. I'm not that far gone." Mona covered her face with her hands. "I'm sorry. I didn't mean that the way it came out." She looked up. "See? That's what I do to Reid all the time - I snap at him and over nothing. He doesn't deserve that." She was on a roll now, the floodgates open on so much she'd been bottling up inside. "I see the way he looks at me now, like he's wondering what he's gotten himself into."

"Is that what he says?"

"No, he's too good to say those words. But he's constantly asking if I'm okay or what's wrong." She looked at Beth, her eyes puddles of moisture. "How am I supposed to answer that when I don't have a clue about either of those things?"

"What exactly worries you?"

"If I can take care of Owen. Before we had him, I knew it's be hard, but I was confident I was up to it, that I'd figure it out and be the best mother to him I could be." Her voice grew smaller. "That was before. Now, I doubt that I can do even his basic care. I worry he's not safe with me." This was really hard, but now that she'd started, it had to come out. "Several times, I don't know how many. Reid's come in the house, and Owen is crying. I'm there, I'm just sitting there, but it's like I'm not. I don't hear Owen. I don't hear Reid until he touches me or gives my arm a shake." She stared into her mug. "He says it scared him. Him and me, both.

"He has to keep quitting his work to come check on us. I think he's afraid I can't look after Owen." Her pleading eyes met Beth's. "I'm afraid of that, too."

The counselor in Beth took over. "Mona, have you had thoughts of hurting yourself?"

Shame, relief and everything in between flashed over Mona's face. Before she could consider the consequences, she nodded.

"Can you tell me about it?"

"I keep thinking how much better off Reid would be without me, Owen would be without me. At least then, Reid would only have himself and his son to look after, not me, as well."

"Have you considered acting on those thoughts?"

Mona shook her head. "I tell myself I'm a coward for not being able to go through with it, and a coward for not sucking it up and just be normal like everyone else."

"Mona, have you ever heard of something called postpartum depression?"

Both women turned their heads as a scraping sound came from near the door.

CHAPTER 26

K eith opened the door for Robin, taking the grocery sack from her arm.

Robin kissed his cheek.

Unpacking the items in the kitchen, Keith wasn't sure how to broach this topic with Robin. Better out with it; Blair was an important part of her life. "The phone rang while you were out."

"Oh, who was it?" Robin pulled a skillet from the drawer beneath the fridge.

"Your son."

"What did he want?"

"I don't know. He didn't leave a message."

"That's odd. Why ever not?"

"I think he was expecting you to answer the phone."

"Well, it is my house he called." Her finger skimmed down the page in her recipe book.

"He seemed unhappy that I answered your phone."

"Why would that be?"

Keith needed her attention. Taking her by the arm, he

turned Robin to face him. "I don't think he's happy that we're spending time with each other."

"Nonsense. It's none of his business and besides, why should he care?"

"Robin, he's your son. Sons are protective of their mothers."

"Yeah, he's always taken on responsibility for everyone; that's his nature. But he doesn't need to protect me - from you, of all people. That's absurd." She turned back to the stove.

Should he let it go? That was his way. Avoid conflict. Be left alone in peace.

Family was important. No matter how many times Izzy tried to explain that, he'd ignored her warning, almost driving Becca away for good. Only breaking his hip so he was unable to work, and Izzy, needing help, pulled Becca away from her shepherding job in England, for the sake of her mother.

He'd almost lost his kid. He wanted no part in that happening to Robin, in her hurting the way he'd never told anyone he had. This was the right thing to do.

Keith reached out to touch Robin, then let his hands drop to his sides. It would be easier without touching her. "Robin, this has been nice."

That got her attention. "Nice? What is nice?"

She was not going to make this easy.

"What we've been doing."

"What exactly *are* we doing? I've been wondering that myself."

"Spending time together. You know what I mean."

Robin just looked at him.

Keith took a deep breath. "Your son is not happy about this."

"This?"

"Us. Seeing each other."

"Why should it matter to him?"

Geez, he hated this touchy-feely stuff. It was Izzy's area, not his.

"He's looking out for you. He's your son, and cares."

"I don't need anyone looking out for me, but me."

Too bad. *He* was going to. "You're his mother and he is concerned about your well-being. He doesn't like me and is not in favor of us hanging out together."

"Last time I looked, I'm an adult, and get to run my own life." Her voice had that testy edge.

"Robin, I know. I get it." He couldn't meet her eyes. "Izzy always lectured me that family comes ahead of everything, and I forgot that for a while. For too long.

"Blair is an important part of your life, and always will be." He waved his hand in the space between them. "Us? Well, this was a pleasant interlude."

"*Interlude!*" Her hands fisted on her hips.

"We're friends. Have been since we were kids; always will be." Leaning forward, Keith gave her a kiss on the forehead. "But we won't be doing this anymore."

He left the kitchen, headed for the front door where he'd left his shoes and coat. "See you at the store tomorrow."

F rom his tractor seat, Reid had a view of the house. Darn. He could see in the back entryway. He'd forgotten to shut the inside door when he left. Although the screen door was shut, it didn't fit well and there could be a draft coming into the kitchen; that could be bad for Owen.

Pulling the throttle back to 1200 rpms, and shifting the levers into neutral and park, he waited two minutes for the turbo chargers to cool, throttled right back, then shut down the tractor. Climbing out, he went up the steps and across the deck to the door.

He paused, his hand on the door's latch, hesitated the same way he had each time he'd entered their home over these last months. It hadn't always been like that; earlier he'd sprinted indoors, eager to see his wife and son. These days, he never knew what he'd find. That didn't mean he didn't want to see them, just that worry got in the way.

But his family was safe right now; Beth was with them, and she'd have called him if anything was wrong.

Except he couldn't hear her voice. Instead, all he heard was Mona. Shouting.

His Mona raising her voice? Calm, easy-tempered, unflappable Mona. At least that *used* to be Mona. Somehow, during these last months, things changed. The next words he heard froze him in place.

"I see the way he looks at me now, like he's wondering what he's gotten himself into."

Who in the world was Mona talking about?

"He's constantly asking if I'm okay or what's wrong. How am I supposed to answer that when I don't have a clue about either of those things?"

Maybe she was talking about him. He was always asking if she was okay. A part of Reid knew he should announce his presence, but this was more of how Mona felt than he'd heard in almost a year. When had they stopped talking to each other, really talking?

Beth said something, but he couldn't catch her soft words. Guess he was more tuned in to Mona, because even though she spoke more quietly now, her words still pierced him.

"Wondering if I can take care of Owen. Before we had him, I knew it'd be hard, but I was confident I was up to it, that I'd figure it out and be the best mother to him I could be.

Now, I doubt I can do even his basic care. I worry he's not safe with me."

Guilt flooded Reid's veins. He hated to admit it even to himself, but he had begun to doubt that, too.

Mona continued. "Several times, I don't know how many. Reid's come in the house, and Owen is crying. I'm there, I'm just sitting there, but it's like I'm not. I don't hear Owen. I don't hear Reid until he touches me or gives my arm a shake."

Oh, he knew those times. They played like a film strip over and over in his mind, like an alternate reality that could not truly be happening.

Mona wasn't finished. Now that Beth had gotten his wife to open the dam, the torrent rushed out. Why would she talk to Beth when he'd begged her to tell him what was going on?

"I think he's afraid I can't look after Owen. I'm afraid of that, too."

Reid removed his work glove and rubbed his eyes. How had they come to this?

With his ear closer to the crack in the door, this time he heard Beth's words. "Mona, have you had thoughts of hurting yourself?"

His heart stopped. His breath caught while he waited for his wife's response.

"I keep thinking how much better off Reid would be without me, and Owen would be without me."

No! The pain in Mona's voice ripped him apart. No! He had lost so many people he loved. That would *not* happen with his beautiful Mona.

Unheeded, his glove dropped to the ground. His chilled fingers fumbled with the metal door latch before yanking it open.

Not caring what his barn boots might track across their floor, he shoved a chair from the end of the kitchen table to beside where Mona sat, her face wet. Sitting, he pulled his wife into his arms, burying her face in his neck, resting his head on hers, clutching to him the most precious thing in his life.

His tears wet her hair, but neither noticed.

Slowly, Beth's words penetrated his senses; she'd repeated them several times.

"Have you ever heard of something called postpartum depression?"

He raised his head and looked at their friend, uncaring that she was seeing him cry. "What? What did you say?"

"I said, have you ever heard of postpartum depression?"

Against his shoulder, Mona shook her head.

"What is that?" He knew what depression was, had experienced it himself after his parents were killed in the accident, then again several years later when his young fiancée died when they were barely out of high school. Those were dark times for him, but he thought they were all behind him now that Mona was in his life.

Beth explained, as if seeing her friends sobbing into each other's arms was an everyday thing. "Most new moms experience 'baby blues' after childbirth, things like mood swings, crying spells, anxiety and difficulty sleeping. That's normal and expected with all the physical and lifestyle changes. It usually goes away within a few weeks.

"But for some women, it lasts much longer and gets worse. Or, it can begin later, during that first year after the birth. I'll have to check, but I think the stats are that about one in ten women who have 'baby blues' go on to have postpartum depression."

"Why?" Reid wanted to know. "There isn't a sunnier person than Mona. She's been through a lot in her life and never had depression."

"I'm not an expert in this field, but I believe it has to do with the social and psychological and chemical changes that happen after the birth.

"After the delivery, there's a rapid drop in hormones. During pregnancy, the body's levels of progesterone and estrogen rise significantly, but they drop sharply after delivery. That swing is hard on a person's body, and can, coupled with the normal fatigue and feelings of overwhelm in caring for a newborn, can bring on depression."

Reid picked Mona up, placing her on his lap, enfolding her once again. He hated to ask this question, but had to know. "Is this…" he swallowed, "permanent?"

"No!" Beth pulled her phone from her pocket. "Hold on a minute while I look something up." She found what she was looking for. "Here are some symptoms of postpartum depression. Mona, do you have any of these:

C rying all the time, often for no reason
  •Depressed mood
  •Being uninterested in your baby
  • Feeling like you're not bonding with your baby
  •Severe anger and crankiness
  •Loss of pleasure
  •Feelings of worthlessness, hopelessness, and helplessness
  •Thoughts of death or suicide
  •Thoughts of hurting someone else
  •Trouble concentrating or making decisions

F or all but one, Mona nodded. She hadn't thought about harming anyone else but herself.

"Guys," continued Beth, "I'm your friend. As such, I cannot make a diagnosis, but you're obviously struggling, and PPD might be the reason."

Reid's eyes pleaded with her. "So, what can we do?"

From the living room came the familiar sounds of a grumpy one-year-old waking up, disgruntled at finding himself all alone.

"I'll get him," Beth offered.

CHAPTER 27

S tunned, Robin stared as her front door clicked shut.
What just happened here?

Had she been dumped?

Not since she was sixteen, and Lloyd Beecher uninvited her to the prom so he could take a cheerleader, had this happened.

Well, that wasn't quite true. There was the time at 19 when her live-in boyfriend ran out on her when she told him she was pregnant. Yeah, there was that. But Ron had taken her in, both her and the yet unborn Blair, raising the baby as his own.

Not since that cowardly boyfriend had a man rejected her.

Had Keith just done this to her? *Keith?*

Sure, they'd known each other since they were children. That made them comfortable with each other. Comfortable was good, right?

Working at his hardware store seemed a natural fit for both of them. Keith needed the help, especially after Izzy passed away. For Robin, well, she needed a new purpose in life, an activity to occupy her time, make her feel useful and a part of something.

That's how it had begun. Keith was not known as the easiest man to get along with. Izzy had had a way with him, but for Robin it took little effort to see past his grumpiness, ignore his grumblings, and manage the aspects of the store he hated to admit he struggled with. They worked well together, even if Keith found it hard to accept some changes she brought about in the store.

Gradually, those changes slid over into their personal lives, as well, but these he didn't appear to mind. From spending eight hours a day in each other's company, it seemed natural to extend those hours into after-work time. After all, they were adults, old friends, and both were alone.

From the odd extended chat after work, to sharing the occasional meal together, over the last year, they'd somehow become a larger part of the other's lives, spending most evenings together.

It had been easy, this transition. Neither of them gave it a name, and certainly the word "dating" never crossed either of their lips.

But Keith was always there. When something in her house or vehicle needed fixing, she no longer called Blair; Keith just took care of it, sometimes noticing the problem before Robin was even aware of it. When Keith grumbled about his daughter, Becca, Robin tried to explain how Becca might feel about things. It pleased her to see the animosity between those two decreasing to levels Izzy would have been so happy to see.

Comfortable. That's how she'd describe what developed between her and Keith. Someone to share a meal with; cooking for two was more fun than making food for just her. Someone companionable to spend time with, to watch a movie together, play backgammon or cribbage. They never went out, both homebodies by nature, but it had been nice having a man hanging around again, sharing day-to-day things with.

Was what they had now the way it would always be? Was it leading to more? Who knew, and neither of them broached the topic.

Had she now lost that?

How? Why?

And what gave Keith the right to make that decision on his own?

What was that nonsense about Blair? Why should Blair care if Keith was at her house? What business was it of his? How dare her son think he had any say in her personal life?

How dare Keith think *he* could decide if they spent time together or not?

Oh, the men in her life.

And what was she supposed to do with the *two* steaks sitting on her kitchen counter?

"What do we do?" Reid repeated his question. Bouncing Owen on her lap, Beth smiled at the baby. "You need to see someone who specializes in postpartum depression."

"Like who?"

"Your family doctor is a start and can recommend a counselor or a psychiatrist."

That brought Mona's head up from Reid's shoulder. "A psychiatrist! I'm not crazy." But it had run through her head lately, wondering if she was.

"Depression is a mental health condition that needs care."

"Like she'll have to go away someplace?" Although he wanted his wife back healthy and happy, being separated even for a while felt too extreme.

Beth shook her head. "I doubt it. Sometimes hospitalization is required, but I would not think it's needed."

"How is this handled?"

"With therapy, or a combination of medication and therapy."

"Therapy?" Mona asked. "Like psychoanalysis? That Freudian stuff?"

"I think cognitive behavior therapy is common for PPD."

"And that is?"

"Ways to look at situations objectively. Changing your thinking about how you perceive things and react. Sometimes we fall into a pattern of faulty or unhelpful thinking and behavior that doesn't get us what we want." Her smile was rueful. "We human beings can be hard on ourselves. CBT can change how we look at things and the ways we respond."

"If it was that easy, then how did I get into such a mess? I used to handle things all right."

"True. But you'd never been pregnant before, never experienced all those changing hormones. Apart from the rapid decrease in progesterone and estrogen right after the baby's birth, there are other hormonal changes." Beth stood up to sway with Owen as he became restless. "You had some difficulties with breastfeeding, didn't you?"

"Thanks for bringing that up," mumbled Mona. "Just another of my failures as a mother."

"Mona! Geez!" Reid pulled back to search his wife's face. "Is that how you see it?"

"How else would you describe a mother who couldn't even feed her own baby?"

"But you did! After that first month, he took better to nursing, and we stopped the bottles."

Mona's words came out muffled against Reid's shirt. "I didn't want to tell you. After a few months of nursing, I kept thinking Owen wasn't getting enough nutrition. I told the nurse practitioner Owen wasn't gaining weight anymore. She suggested I give him formula during the day, just nursing him first thing in the morning and at night."

"Why didn't you tell me?" asked Reid. "I could have been helping you with that."

"A mother is supposed to feed her child."

"But..."

Beth interrupted the couple. "There are lactogenic hormones, like oxytocin and prolactin, implicated in postpartum depression. They regulate things like the production and secretion of breast milk, but influence maternal mood and behavior as well. They, along with other hormones, may not be at optimal levels in your body right now."

"So, they can give her some of these hormones?" Reid asked.

"I don't know. That would be up to her doctor. I also think the thyroid gland's production sometimes has something to do with postpartum depression, so they'll probably check that, too."

"Sounds like our doctor is the first step."

Beth agreed with Reid. "Sometimes antidepressants are prescribed."

"But..." began Mona, looking at her son. "I'm still breastfeeding, at least a little."

"There are some antidepressants that are safe to take while nursing." She crossed to the kitchen counter. "More coffee anyone? I want some." Replenishing their mugs, she replaced the coffee carafe. "Even with medication, they usually recommend some type of therapy to learn new coping strategies to manage the symptoms."

"Can I get better?"

"Yes. Definitely, your life can get better. I should warn

you, though, not instantly. Most medications take a while to get into your system before you can feel the effects - maybe up to two weeks. And patterns and ways of thinking don't turn around right away. It'll take time to change them, but talking about it helps."

"It already has. This last while's been awful, feeling like I have to hide this mammoth, black secret, and pretend to the world that I'm okay."

"Mona." Reid put his lips to her ear. "Never pretend. Tell me, tell me anything. We can get through it together if I only know what's going on."

"I couldn't tell you what was going on when I didn't understand it myself. I hated disappointing you, and disappointing myself."

"You could never do that."

"When we brought the baby home, I wanted everything to be perfect for us."

Beth cleared her throat. "Remember that faulty thinking thing I mentioned? Perfect doesn't enter into any of this with us humans. We're not perfect and trying to be makes us feel like failures."

"Tell me about it," Mona mumbled.

Reid stood up, placing his wife back in her own chair.

"Where are you going?" Mona asked.

"I'm making an appointment with Dr. Hunter. You okay with that?"

CHAPTER 28

R obin stared at herself in her bathroom mirror. Why was she fussing with her hair today? She was a two-minute gal - that's all the time she'd allow herself to spend on hair in the morning. And that was on the days she washed her hair; other days, it was comb and go, or a scrunchie.

She'd even added mascara to her eyelashes, something she did only a few times a year. Which reminded her - she needed to buy more. This tube was almost dried up and left clumps. Staring at her reflection, she pulled a few more globs of dried mascara lumps stuck to her lashes. A sixty-year-old who still had not learned how to apply eye makeup with any finesse.

Enough. She was too old to be spending this much time worrying about her appearance. So why was she? Not even when Keith had been coming over every evening had she thought about how she looked, or what she wore. He never seemed to care, and neither did she.

She was not trying to impress him. Of course not.

There was no good reason it was taking her so long to get

dressed and ready this morning. She hated fussbudgets, and now she was acting like one. Enough!

P ulling into her usual parking spot in the alley behind the hardware store, Robin took a minute to compose herself. For what? This was ridiculous. Why so nervous?

Was it because of Keith? Him dumping her? She winced at her choice of words. He'd called what they'd been doing an 'interlude' and that it was over. Why should she care?

Why was she sitting there like a ninny? Someone would've heard her car drive up and think something was wrong because she didn't come in right away.

Something felt wrong. She just wasn't sure what. Why so off kilter? What had changed since she was at work last week?

Keith. The only thing different was that Keith would not be coming around to her place anymore.

So what? She had gotten along just fine without him prior to this last year. Prior to the last six decades, in fact.

She was an independent woman. Secure. Confident.

Just like that time in high school, when she held her head high and showed that stupid Lloyd Beecher boy that she didn't care, she would do the same thing now.

No way would she be a victim to Keith's whims. She had a little house she liked. She had her son, and now a daughter-in-law and two foster granddaughters she adored. She had her stake in the farm, plus a job she enjoyed. What more could anyone ask for?

It took another three deep breaths before she opened her door. Just as she did, Mona and Owen drove up beside her.

Perfect. Just the distraction she needed. Becca wasn't working this morning, so the only person who might have noticed her sitting out here working up the courage to go in was Keith. His hearing wasn't the best, so he might not have even heard her arrive. Just as well.

Glancing up, she saw the store's back door was open, and Keith emerged wearing his boots and a coat. How long had he been there? It was his habit to meet Mona when she drove up, helping her carry in Owen and the baby's things. Although these days there was less to tote around since Keith had bought replicas of some of the baby's things to keep at the store.

Keith's eyes met hers. Busted! She knew him well, and his look told her he knew of her reluctance to see him. Robin straightened her spine and met his look with a level gaze, her chin jutting out just the slightest. Who cared what he thought?

Keith gave her a gentle smile. "Morning." Then his attention turned to little Owen.

Robin had never taken Keith for a baby type of guy. True, during Owen's first week at the store, Keith kept his distance, but when no one was looking, Keith spent more and more time crouched by the child, making faces at him through the fence, tirelessly retrieving the toys Owen tossed outside of his pen. Then, giving in to the child's raised arms and pleading eyes, Keith lifted him into his arms. After that, Owen spent a considerable chunk of his time being carried around the store by Keith, drooling on the man, pulling off his glasses, and demanding attention.

So the guy had a soft spot for children. Didn't make him a saint. Didn't make him someone she wanted to spend time with.

But she did. If Robin allowed herself to be honest, she missed the old coot. Seeing him at work every day was not the same as seeing him alone in her house. At the store, there were always other people around, and they need to behave as a professionals in a work place. At her house though, they'd let all that go, relaxing and being themselves. Sometimes they played a game or watched television, or talked. Sometimes they didn't, and that was okay, too. Keith never minded if she pulled out her knitting, or a book. He perused wood-working magazines he brought over, then kept at her place.

That reminded her - she'd need to gather them up and give them back to him. Should that include the one she'd subscribed for him for Christmas, or the others he'd subscribed to, having them sent to her address? He'd said, "Here's where I read them, so I might as well have them come here."

They'd been comfortable together, almost like an old married couple.

CHAPTER 29

How long was that woman going to sit out there Keith wondered. Was Robin going to quit her job? Was she so ticked with him she couldn't face him? It'd only been two days, well, two-and-a-half, since he'd last walked out of her house. A long two days, very long.

He was used to being alone. Not that he necessarily liked it, but it had been two years since his Izzy died, so he'd had time to get used to it. The silence of being in the house alone, not just the absence of sound, but the lack of the essence of the person, the partner he'd lived with for so long, was what he felt most. The impulse to turn to his spouse to share a comment came less frequently now, not that he hadn't done that often enough, but the lack of a reply eventually penetrated, and then saturated his gut. Each time, it would hurt, at first like a deep knife stab reminding him of what he'd lost. Over time, those stabs turned to nicks, pocketknife-sized, still poignant, but the pain was not as deep as at first.

Those first months he woke up in the bed alone, not even a crease in the other pillow. No sound of the shower running, nor the spitting of the coffee maker. Izzy always made the coffee. He'd bought a new coffee machine, one with a timer that would start brewing before he was even out of bed. Mona, dear girl, had programmed it for him, so that all he had to do was dump in the water and grounds, then push a button and it would work its magic automatically each morning. Maybe a bit ridiculous, but he'd taken pride in doing that for himself after so many years of relying on Izzy to make the coffee.

Mona was easy; he had not dared ask Becca to help him with this. He annoyed her enough already.

True, he was needy after Izzy died. What did they expect? He was an old man, and useless in the kitchen. At least, that's what Izzy always said, plus they both much preferred her cooking to his own.

Soon after her mother's death, Becca expected him to suddenly know his way around a kitchen. The girl had no idea; that had been Izzy's domain, and she didn't appreciate anyone else messing it up.

So what if Becca put meals into individual packages and stuck them in his freezer? Did she think he'd gnaw away at the frozen meat? Yeah, he could see that it took her some time to make up all those packages, but how did you get them from the freezer to the plate? Becca tried. He had to hand it to his girl for that. She tried explaining and demonstrating, but she had no concept of the mess his head was in right after his Izzy died.

It was like his brain froze. Very little penetrated, other than the fact that Izzy was no longer there, no longer by his side, no longer anywhere. Life as he'd known it was over. Just gone.

Maybe if they'd known this was coming, maybe if there'd been some warning. But would he have wanted her to suffer? To be incapacitated? No way, not Izzy, who never stayed still.

There was a guy they knew in town, a vibrant man who loved fishing and hunting and camping, spent every minute doing something. Until his first heart attack. The subsequent ones left him a little worse off each time, more incapacitated, more bound to his chair, and a lifestyle he detested.

No, that was not what he would have wanted for his Izzy, even if it meant he'd still have her by his side.

Despite Becca's frustration with him, his inability to do more than move from bed to couch and back in those initial weeks, he thought he'd done better than would many men. Not right away, of course, but over the months. If a guy was a chatterbox, suddenly having no one to talk to would be worse. Luckily, he wasn't that guy, wasn't gabby, and didn't mind periods of quiet. Thank goodness Izzy understood that. He needed down time, time to himself, and so had she. It worked out; they were good together.

Not just husband and wife, but friends. Companions. In sync.

They shared not just a life, but a purpose, building this business. They'd taken it from what his father had, and expanded until it was what it is today - a vital, respected part of the community.

He still had that. If not for the girls, he could have lost his hardware store in those blank months after Izzy's death. Becca and Mona stepped up to cover for him. Robin, too. She'd increased her hours from part-time to full-time. The women had insured that his business continued when he faltered, then coaxed him back to life.

A part of him had been ashamed of his weakness, ashamed that he fell to pieces, but those around him either pretended not to see how frail he was, or, as Robin said over and over, it was normal.

Normal? Not for him. Nothing about this was normal.

Robin said the same thing happened to her after Ron

died, but Keith didn't remember. Oh, he'd attended the funeral, of course; the four of them had known each other since childhood. But visiting the widow afterward? Nope. He left stuff like that to Izzy.

He recalled Izzy coming home from some of those visits, telling him how hard this was for Robin, even once Blair got back home. He had paid little attention to what his wife was saying.

It was different when it happened to him. How did you survive, let alone recover from losing your best friend, the person who got you, who knew you sometimes better than you knew yourself? He'd always considered himself a self-sufficient guy, but oh, he was so wrong about that after losing Izzy. She was a part of him, a jigsaw where their edges merged perfectly and welded together, making him whole, a better, more complete person.

With those parts of him ripped out, it had taken time to get his legs back under him, time to emerge from that dark hole where it felt like life was over. He knew Becca thought he took too long. But what did she know? She hadn't just lost the best part of her. Yeah, Izzy had been her mother, but Becca was grown now. The two of them hadn't even lived together for over a decade. Losing your mom was far different from losing your spouse.

When he'd grumbled about that, Robin chided him. Loss was loss, and you could not categorize one as harder than the other. You never knew what was in the heart of someone else.

Over time, he'd realized the world hadn't ended, and life wasn't over, but different. He didn't have to like this difference, this new way of being, but it was what it was.

There was a fine line between grieving and feeling sorry for yourself. Too often, Keith knew he slipped over into the latter. Not a pretty picture, not one he wanted to think about. Instead, he snarled, mostly at Becca, as he plunged into the abyss where life wasn't fair.

Now, only sometimes did that darkness try to overtake him.

It had this weekend.

CHAPTER 30

"Let me take that little guy," Keith told Mona as he approached her car. "He's getting too heavy for you." Had hoisting Becca into the air when she was this age given him this same thrill? He couldn't remember. Maybe it was too long ago, over thirty years. Or was Becca right when she complained he never had time for her as a child, never understood her? Izzy was there for those sorts of things; they each did what they were good at. Izzy did more of the child-rearing, and he concentrated on providing a living for his family.

Mona knew it was useless to argue as Keith plucked Owen from her arms, striding away with her son. She smiled a greeting at Robin.

"What can I help you carry in?" Robin already had Mona's car's back door open, reaching for the diaper bag.

"If you can take that, I have some baking in the trunk I thought we could have at our coffee break."

. . .

K ids were a good thing, thought Keith. They provided a focus for people, a good focus.

He'd stood at the back door for over five minutes, wondering if Robin was going to sit in her car all day or come in. Was she thinking of quitting? Had she had enough of him?

He knew he was not the easiest man in the world. Becca told him that constantly, and so had Izzy, but in a different way. His wife had loved him anyway, while he irritated his daughter to no end. Sometimes he felt the same way about her, but more and more of the time what he felt for Becca was regret.

He noticed how easy Robin was with her son, and now her daughter-in-law. He saw how Becca's husband, Stan, interacted with his parents and wished he could be for Stan the kind of in-law Phoebe and Jim were to Becca.

Robin had helped. When he groused about something Becca had said or done, she explained to him how things might look from Becca's lens.

People were messy.

That's why he preferred to retreat into himself, follow what interested him, learn new things. Facts were clean and clear; people were not.

He used to have Izzy to run interference for him, but not anymore. Robin told him he'd have to learn to figure it out on his own, or die a lonely old man.

Apart from Izzy, he'd never thought he needed people. Maybe he did.

What he felt this past weekend didn't have a label, or at least one he cared to admit. Was Robin right, and he was a lonely old man?

Old was a relative term. To the kids, yeah, he was old. But in his early sixties, he might live another thirty years.

That stopped him. His parents had lived well into their eighties and nineties. That was a long time, a long time to be alone.

Being alone was okay. He'd made peace of a sort with it the long year after Izzy died. He never questioned if he was happy; he just was what he was.

But then, things had changed. These past months, somehow, he was lighter. He caught himself smiling more. Looking forward to things more.

Mostly, what he looked forward to was spending time with Robin.

Now that was over.

Leaning down, Keith settled Owen in his pen, catching the child's interest in some of his squeaky toys.

It paid to plan ahead. Since sleep had proved elusive in the early morning hours today, he'd gotten up, and planned out his delivers. By the time the sun crept over the horizon, his truck was loaded and ready for him to get on the road just as soon as Robin or Mona arrived to look after the store.

First to arrive had been Robin. The way she remained in her car, checking herself in her rearview mirror, she was no more eager to see him than he was to see her.

No, that wasn't true. Something in his heart sped up when he saw her car turn into the alley. No matter how much he told himself he'd done the right thing, it still felt wrong. But, upsetting Robin's son was not worth any pleasure he himself might get out of Robin's company. Family came first. He could see that now, even though he might not have acted that way when Becca was younger. He couldn't go back and fix that, but he could make sure he didn't interfere with Robin's relationship with her son.

. . .

The women entered the store, the wafting aroma of baking coming with them. He doubted Robin felt warm and fuzzy enough toward him right now to bake for him, so it must have been Mona. A great young woman, although sometimes she looked sad. Today, though, she smiled at him, a smile that touched not only her lips, but her eyes.

"Smells great, ladies." Keith took a peek inside the plastic container. He pretended to scowl at Owen. "Don't you dare eat them all, little man. Save some for me." Turning to the women, he said, "I'm off on some deliveries. Might not be back this morning." He headed for the back door, relieved at not having to look directly at Robin or say anything to her.

Cowardly? Maybe, but that was the way it was.

CHAPTER 31

Mona had only been on this medication for a week, but already some of the cloud seemed to lift. It had been months since she'd taken any interest in preparing food, but yesterday she'd baked up a storm. Just the act of filling the house with wonderful aromas raised her spirits and made her feel more capable than she'd been in a long time.

It helped that almost every day now someone dropped in even for just an hour to help with Owen, offer her a break, or just to chat. The guys came by too, and helped Reid with the cattle, giving him more time to be inside with his wife and son. Each little piece helped, and Mona no longer tried to hide from her friends or chase them away.

Sometimes she visited with them; sometimes not. They got it without her trying to turn herself inside out, explaining. A walk alone, a leisurely bath, a nap, or even losing herself in a book for half an hour restored her spirits. Oh, how she appreciated her friends and family. What on earth had stopped her from asking them for help before?

It was part of depression, Beth told her - that feeling of

everything being too much trouble, the fear of what someone might think, that gnawing ache of not being good enough. Yeah, those feelings were still there, just maybe not as intense before. Plus now, Reid helped. He seemed to understand when to override her objections to having someone around, and when to respect that she simply needed to be alone.

Beth bought her a journal - two of them, in fact. The plain, lined one with the soft leather cover was for her to write in, write any thoughts that came to her, the good ones and the dark ones. No one else need ever read them, not even Mona herself, if she didn't want to.

The other notebook was more of a day-timer with lines for each hour of the day. In this one, Mona wrote down how she spent her day, what she did with Owen and, what she did around the house. This book she shared with Beth.

Her friend helped her see that, while it felt like she was useless to both Reid and Owen, actually, she did get stuff done. She was not the total loser mother and wife her brain told her she was. Sure, she was not perfect, not by a long shot, and nowhere near the efficient Mona she had once been, but she was not a nothing, and there was a good chance she'd get back to being her former self.

She clutched that hope and held on.

Winter was a time for planning for farmers. What to plant in each field next spring, the variety of each crop, how much fertilizer to use, which herbicides might be needed. There was a lot to consider, each decision having the potential to create profit or loss.

While Reid and Blair scratched figures on papers strewn across the kitchen table, debating the merits of buying pricey new wheat seed that was supposed to yield five percent higher, Friday and Randine babysat Owen in Reid's living room. For the girls, it had been a toss up - play with the baby, or go visit Becca's alpacas. The baby won out, at least this time.

At 15, Friday was certainly old enough to babysit both Owen and her younger sister, Randine. But Mona worried, as would all new mothers. For many people experiencing postpartum depression, anxiety compounded the problem, consuming the parent with worry and panicky feelings.

Although she didn't feel lucky, Mona had the depression part, but only experienced mild anxiety, and showed no signs of the more severe part of the spectrum, postpartum psychosis.

Still, she worried, or maybe fretted was a better description. It had nothing to do with not liking nor trusting Friday. The worry was a free-floating thing, hard to grab hold of and clarify, but the sertraline medication helped relieve some of both the depression and the anxiety.

Two months ago, she would never have considered leaving the house. Now things were easier. Mona trusted Reid, knowing he'd do anything for their son. So, as long as Reid remained in the house, she consented to Friday spending the afternoon with Owen.

That meant she was free, one of those times she'd come to relish. Today was Beth's idea. One day after school that week, Robin picked up Friday and Randine, driving them to Becca's farm. Two alpacas had given birth, their crias adorable, and the girls were in love with the creatures.

Now it was Mona's turn.

Things had changed since she'd last been here. Blair created a rustic wooden sign now displayed prominently over the front door, letting all who entered know the quality of the crafts they were about to see in Becca's new on-farm store.

. . .

S weat equity had built the place. Becca inherited the land and old farmhouse from her grandparents. Sort of.

When the great grandparents died, the land passed on to Keith's father. Allergic to grain dust, pollen and animal dander, Keith's dad rarely stepped foot on the land. As a small boy, Keith relished the time he got to spend with his grandparents on their farm, but the risk of bringing home allergens limited the times Keith was allowed free rein on that land.

On Keith's grandparents' passing, they had rented the land out to local farmers. When his father died, Keith carried on with how his parents handled the land, in recent years renting it to Stan.

When the pressures and bullying of high school got to be too much, teenaged Becca would head out to her grandparents' farm. The renters only wanted the arable land for crops and hay; they didn't care about the decaying yard site. Becca spent countless hours wandering the yard, finding remnants of the garden and orchard her great grandmother had tended.

Despite her father's warnings to never venture inside the neglected and decrepit buildings, Becca did. She came to love the old farmhouse with its carved newel posts, the wide wooden floorboards, the bayed kitchen window overlooking the pasture. She'd climb the stairs, inspecting each room, deciding which one she'd claim for her own one day.

And she had.

When Keith fell and broke his hip, it did not heal well after the surgery. Izzy had her hands full trying to look after her husband, plus keep their hardware store going on her own. It could not be done.

So she asked Becca to come home and help. Becca, who vowed never to return to the town that had caused her nothing but grief in school, to a father she'd never seen eye to eye with. But she loved her mother enough to give up her job as a shepherdess in England, and travel back across the ocean.

Izzy knew her daughter well. Keith assumed Feldman's Hardware would pass on to Becca, the third generation, to uphold the name and the store. It was a given - his father had expected it of him, now his child would take up the mantle.

"It's not in the cards," Izzy told her husband. "She may have grown up working here, and is back now to help us, but this is *your* dream, not Becca's. Our girl needs to follow her heart."

"And just where is that heart leading her?" Keith wanted to know.

"I'm not sure, but it might have something to do with animals. And land." Izzy knew the way to keep Becca near was to give her land and the freedom to do with it what she would.

CHAPTER 32

B eth and Mona joined Becca at the fence alongside the alpaca pen. Counting the babies and the sires, the herd now numbered almost a dozen animals.

"I hope to have twice as many by this time next year," Becca told her friends.

"How's the store going?"

Beth kept her smile to herself, pleased that Mona had asked. It was a sign of Mona coming back to life, taking in an interest in her friends.

"Better than I hoped. The first week was iffy, but once word spread, things picked up. Now my biggest problem is keeping enough inventory on the shelves."

"What's your biggest seller?"

"Socks. Alpaca wool socks, with mittens a close second. I'm getting faster at knitting them, but it still takes time when I'm looking after these animals, minding the store, and helping out at the hardware store." She gave them a grin. "But it's good to be busy, right?"

"You make me feel like a slacker," admitted Beth. "I only have my job and the girls and house. Robin's teaching me how to knit, though. My family will tolerate my first efforts, but eventually I'll get good enough to make socks for your store."

"Thanks. Much appreciated. Your mother-in-law is a knitting machine."

"She said it made an enormous difference using the needles your dad created for her."

"Yeah, he gave me a similar set for my birthday last month." The most personalized gift he'd ever given Becca. In fact, it was the only present she could remember receiving from him. Growing up, her mother took care of picking out gifts for birthdays and Christmas.

The knitting needles would have taken countless hours to make, let alone the specialized case designed to hold them. Maybe it wasn't unusual for a father to spend so much time on a gift for his only child, at least in a normal family. But to do that for Robin? "What do you think is up with that, Dad devoting so much time to make something for Robin?"

Blair had asked Beth the same thing. Numerous times. "One way to look at it is he knew he'd be helping *you* by providing Robin with better tools to make products for your store."

"Maybe." Could be true, but he wasn't known for assisting his daughter with anything that didn't fall in with *his* plans.

"Or, it could be he enjoys doing things with his hands, and this was a project he thought of." Somehow, but it didn't quite feel right. "Another possibility is that he wanted to do something sweet for Robin."

"Why?"

Exactly what Blair kept asking. "They're old friends, known each other since childhood. They're both alone now, and so might enjoy each other's company."

"*Dad's* company?" Becca could not understand how

anyone could. "Mom was a saint putting up with that man. Hard to see how anyone else could stand him."

That was more along the lines of how Blair felt. "I find your dad sweet, in a gruff sort of way. Once you look past that, he's a softy, Beth replied."

Becca rolled her eyes.

Mona joined in. "When I first started working at the hardware store, he scared me. I'd had grumpy bosses before though, so I knew I could stick it out. At first, your mom ran interference, but then I started to get to know Keith and realized his insides were all marshmallow goo. He's been good to me, and you should see him with Owen. He's gaga over that child."

"Yeah, I've noticed. I hate to admit this, but at first I was almost jealous of Owen. Never can I remember him being that way over me as a child, or even paying attention to me, other than to criticize."

"I wonder if he was focused on making a living for his family back then, and that took all his energy. Izzy told me that the store struggled for many years." As someone who'd been the sole financial support for her own family for years, Mona understood that kind of worry and what it could do to a person.

"Maybe," Becca said, "but it doesn't give him the excuse for being so grouchy all the time."

"You know, your mom and I spent a lot of time together while Keith recovered from his hip surgery," Mona said. "Izzy noticed when Keith was gruff with me. I tried to put it down to the fact that he was in pain, and not take it personally. Izzy explained how Keith pushed people away."

Becca snorted. "No kidding! Pushed me halfway around the world."

"Your mom's explanation was that Keith was leery of what people might ask of him."

"That's his job! Customers ask him stuff all the time."

"That's work-related. Izzy said Keith was wary of people invading his personal space, of what they might ask of him emotionally. It was easier to push people away than to risk being vulnerable to them - him needing them, or others asking more of him than he was willing to give."

"Except for mom."

Mona smiled. "Yeah, it was cute seeing them together. Gruff old Keith would do anything for his wife.

"Anything except be a real father to their daughter." Becca could not keep the bitterness from her voice. That was okay; her friends were well aware of the animosity between Becca and her dad. The whole town knew.

"Do you think he's softening now?" Beth thought she'd noticed signs.

"Dad? No way! It's not in him." The words came out on autopilot. Stan was always telling her to give her father a chance, that he didn't find Keith such a bad old coot. That the guy might be lonely and trying to make things right. To be fair, Stan might have a point. "He comes out here sometimes."

When Becca first took over the land, her father would hardly look at her, let alone step foot out here. "He still has it in his head that I'll take over Feldman's Hardware, no matter how many times I tell him no way. There is the odd morning though, when I come out to feed the alpacas to find it's already been taken care of, and dad is petting one of them. And when we were working on the house, he came out some evenings and Sundays with his tools and got to work. Never said much, didn't grouse, just pitched in."

After being abandoned for decades, the old farmhouse had been in rough shape. Blair applied his carpentry skills, determining that the structure's bones were sound. He and Stan started with the roof, replacing a few sagging rafters, and re-shingling the building. Next, they removed all the old, decaying siding, replacing it with new, and adding energy-efficient windows.

Once the outside was weatherproof, they tackled the interior, removing the old lath and plaster walls, updating the wiring, plumbing and heat ducting. Next came new drywall, wall paint, then flooring. Along the way, they altered interior walls and the space to suit both personal living, and a store to sell alpaca products, crafts, preserves, and fresh produce in the future.

They'd taken things a step at a time, first getting the kitchen, an upstairs bedroom and bathroom ready so Becca and Stan could move in. It helped that Beth was a former interior designer, and Blair a journeyman carpenter, plus all the cousins were handy with tools, so most of the work was a labor of love.

Although such projects were never totally completed, everything was operational now. And yes, Keith had come out more and more, it seemed, quietly helping his daughter with her dream.

CHAPTER 33

It was one of those rare days when all three women worked at the hardware store together. In the lull between customers, Becca, Robin and Mona surveyed the space.

A lot had changed over the last few years, much of it against Keith's wishes. The place had been laid out the same for decades. For much of that time, only Izzy had her finger on where everything was. Organized? Not to anyone else, but Izzy remembered precisely where she'd set each item, even if it had found its resting place years ago.

That didn't work so badly when it was just Izzy and Keith. The man relied on his wife to find anything he or a customer required. But when Keith's injury kept him from working in the store, Becca returned home.

After being in Europe for years, she was unfamiliar with where things were in the store. And, since Becca started her own enterprise on her farm, she could only spend part time hours at the hardware store.

That's where Mona came in as a new hire. Her help meant that Izzy could divide her time between the store and looking after her fretful husband as he recovered and gradually regained mobility.

With Izzy preoccupied, Becca and Mona got to work rearranging the store. Now, all the painting related products were in one section as opposed to being here and there, and everyone was not reliant on Izzy for being able to find items.

Although re-organizing the place took months, most of it done when neither Keith nor Izzy were around, that was only the start of the changes. The paper record keeping system her parents used made no sense to Becca. Order forms and inventory sheets were constantly misplaced, and too much relied on memory.

After Becca and Mona looked into options, they purchased and began using a computerized inventory system. They waited until it was up and running smoothly before showing Becca's parents. Keith walked away, not even willing to give it a chance. Izzy tried to be patient with the girls, but much preferred her pencil-and-paper system.

Since Izzy's death, only Keith remained glued to a paper system, keeping the ordering sheets in a jumbled pile on the shelf under the cash register. Did they get lost? You bet. But the digital copies remained on the computer, backed up to the cloud each night.

Although Becca had little influence over her father, somehow, Robin did. It would be a stretch to say Keith never grumped at Robin, but he did it less frequently and more quietly than he ever did with Becca. Slowly, he was relinquishing his hold on ordering supplies. He would never admit it, but with Becca, Robin, and Mona in charge of the orders, their shelves were stocked more consistently. And, because of the way things were organized now, even he could find items without having to ask for help.

· · ·

K eith was in the storage room. Who knew if he was doing something essential to the running of the hardware store or if he was puttering? He might've thought it a well-kept secret, but all the women in his life knew that he used that storage room to escape when he wanted time for himself. Since there were others now to mind the front of the store, he retreated to his private space more often.

In behind a stack of paint cans, he had a well-hidden library of how-to magazines. At least he had *thought* his stash a well-kept secret until the collection increased a while ago. All the magazines and journals he had kept at Robin's house suddenly joined the others in his hiding spot.

It hit him harder than he imagined. Memories of those evenings spent with Robin in her house. Her reading or knitting while he studied the magazines. The competitive games of backgammon (he almost always won), or cribbage (Robin the clear champion) they played. Watching movies with his arm around her, the faint floral scent of her hair when her head rested on his shoulder.

And now how did he spend his evenings? Alone on his couch in the small living space behind the store. It was familiar, but cluttered. Izzy had liked to make piles of things she planned to put away later. Later never seemed to arrive, and the piles grew. It was a system similar to how Izzy stocked the hardware store. It was Izzy's way, and he'd never questioned it.

Since his wife's death, he could not bear to sort through her things. Becca had given away most of her mother's clothes, but his growls kept her away from removing anything from the living room.

This was home and had been for most of their married life. It was simply what it was, and he'd never given it a thought. That is until he started spending time at Robin's.

There was something relaxing about being in an uncluttered space, where things were tidy, but not too tidy for comfort. In Robin's living room, there were only two piles - one in a wicker basket on an end table, storing her knitting patterns and current project. On the table at the other end of the couch was a matching basket holding a pile of his magazines.

He wondered what was in that basket now? Was it filled with her things, or did she have another gentleman friend now claiming that space as his own?

Nope, he would not go there. No way was he going to think about that possibility, and most certainly he'd never ask her.

The magazines - focus on the magazines instead.

Most of them covered aspects of fine woodworking, but he was eclectic. Most recently, his interest was in learning about welding junkyard art. Who would've thought that was a thing? But apparently it was, and they sold well at craft fairs.

Used to keeping his thoughts to himself, Keith never mentioned to anyone, not even Robin, his interest in trying his hand at building such creations out of junk and scrap metal. So far, it was just a dream. How could he weld in the tiny room behind the main part of the hardware store? Maybe one day...

CHAPTER 34

Alone in the store one evening, Keith studied the set of rustic shelves by the hardware store's picture window, a recently added section of the store, graced by a carved wooden plaque saying 'Alpaca Haven'. It was a scaled-down replica of the mammoth sign Blair had made for Becca to hang above the entrance to her store on the farm.

Now, a small sampling of some of what Becca's Alpaca Haven sold was on display in Feldman's Hardware. Not a lot, but some hand knit mittens, hats, scarves and socks, some preserves and crafts, and wooden toys Blair had made in his spare time.

Visible from the window, these items brought foot traffic into the store with customers lingering, buying, and asking about what else they'd find at Alpaca Haven.

Was Keith on board with this? "No way are you bringing crafts into a hardware store. We sell *hardware*. What don't you get about that?"

"Dad, we could do some quid pro quo. Your customers would be interested in seeing what Alpaca Haven is all about.

If you chose some hardware items that fit with some crafts we sell at the farm, and then stocked them at *my* store, it would be advertising and some extra sales for Feldman's Hardware."

As if oblivious to his protests, Robin, Becca, and Mona disregarded his orders and went ahead with the swap, anyway. Since he refused to have anything to do with the foolish notion, Robin picked items from his store to display at Alpaca Haven. She started with woodworking and finishing tools that complimented some crafts Blair and other woodworkers made to sell on consignment. Later, she added soap-making kits, something he didn't even know they carried. Becca had slipped them into the orders, along with bee keeping equipment. Now, in his paint section, there were stencils, sponges, and other things he didn't know how to use, but Mona said were used to make designs on walls. She'd even hung small patches of drywall, demonstrating various techniques. It was Robin who insisted that they carry a range of sealing jars and canning equipment.

Again, they ignored his protests. Maybe that was just as well because these items sold and sold well. There was no need to congratulate the three of them on their choices; that would just make them think they could continue to ride roughshod over him, forgetting that this was *his* store.

I n one area of the hardware store, the women had arranged displays of knitting, jams, jellies, soaps and candles. On nights like this, when no one else was around, Keith inspected the Alpaca Haven display in his store, noting that it was ever changing; people were buying things.

Although he'd never admit it to anyone, when alone, he taught himself to use the new-fangled computer system so he could see how much money Becca's tomfoolery actually

brought in. Plus, he could see the money *his* items out at
Alpaca Haven garnered.

Maybe he'd been hasty in objecting to this idea. It *was*
benefitting both of them.

He ran his hand over one of the wooden toys carved by
Blair, the workmanship impeccable. Rubbing his fingers over
the satiny finish, Keith could imagine the wood shavings
falling around his feet as the creation came to life, the sweet
scent of cedar, the rhythmic rasp of fine sandpaper shaping
the object smooth. What if *he* could make such things, too?

Fanciful notion. Where in the world could he do anything
like that? Set up on the counter in the hardware store, filling
the place with sawdust? That would never work.

The kitchen? There was barely enough counter space to
prepare a meal or throw a can of whatever in a pot. The
kitchen table was covered in items too large to fit in the
cupboards.

The back room? Never. He gave up the struggle to try to
use the miniature lathe in there to make pens. There simply
was not enough space.

He thought about the wood working tools he'd
optimistically purchased over the years, most still pristine in
their original packaging. Somehow, he'd thought that he'd
have time, have space, to do something with them. It had
never happened, and likely never would.

He picked up another of Blair's creations, a wooden truck
of laminated wood, with moving parts. Even the steering
wheel turned, and the tailgate flipped open when the truck
box tilted to dump its imaginary load. The young man was
good, very good, although Robin said he had limited tools.
Would he be even better if he had access to some of the
equipment in Keith's storage room?

CHAPTER 35

E ven though she wasn't scheduled to work until that afternoon, Robin came in early. It was the phone call from Becca that did it, the enthusiasm in her voice as she shared what she and Mona had discussed.

Revenue from the shelves dedicated to Alpaca Haven products rose steadily. What if they could use more space in the hardware store?

Becca and Mona did their best to reorganize inventory, but it just didn't work. Shuffling a deck of cards resulted in the same number of cards occupying the same amount of space; so it was with their efforts to create more floor or shelf room in the store. Hence the call to Robin to see if she had any ideas.

She did, but this was something best discussed in person.

W hen Robin arrived, Mona was on the computer, searching their inventory program.

"She's trying to find items that don't sell well, so we could put them on sale, then clear them out of the hardware store to make more room," Becca explained.

"I'm not coming up with much of anything," Mona said. "We already streamlined the inventory, getting rid of things that hung around too long. Most of what we have now turns over reasonably well."

It had been Robin to first think of eliminating poor sellers after noticing that once she removed the dust and ages of old grime from some items, the tins showed signs of rust. Keith had no idea how long the things had sat on those shelves. "Izzy would know," was his only response.

"But we can't sell cans that are in this shape," Robin said.

He had shrugged and walked away.

Stan helped the women load his truck with the damaged goods, along with glues that had long since hardened, and chemicals that had been banned years ago. With those disposed of, the shelves were less cluttered, but by now, all that should be removed had already gone.

The storage room was basically a large walk-in closet with floor to ceiling shelves along three sides. Stacked shelves, capable of holding no more. The effort of retrieving anything from that room was like playing a game of hopscotch, jumping over the cases stored on the floor, balancing on one foot to reach things tucked in corners. There simply was not enough room.

Robin needed to check something out before she shared her idea with Becca and Mona. "Be right back," she told them.

Leaving the main part of the store, Robin entered the living area at the rear of the building. Yep, same cramped living room, with too much furniture for the size of the space. A narrow hallway led to the galley-style kitchen where Keith stood at the stove, heating a can of soup.

Hmph, Robin thought. The best he can do is a boughten

can of tomato soup? She'd shown him how to make that from scratch - he'd even helped her that time.

Ripe juicy tomatoes fresh from the garden; shallots and pearl onions from that same garden, caramelizing in butter, churned from Clarabelle's milk, basil snipped from the herbs growing above her kitchen sink, the aromas mingling as Keith chopped the tomatoes. The Chianti he'd brought paired well with the soup when it finished simmering. It made a fine meal, along with the charcuterie board or meats, cheeses and crackers.

After *that* he could go back to canned soup? Obviously. The man was incapable of recognizing when he had it good.

Hearing footsteps, Keith turned toward the sound, a wooden spoon in his hand. He couldn't help it, he stared at the woman who had been occupying his thoughts. She looked better than ever, her silvery hair catching the sunlight from the transom window at the end of the hall, her head tilted at that saucy angle, her chin pointing at him.

But her eyes, oh, they had changed. These were not the eyes of the woman who cuddled against him on her couch after sharing a meal together, nor the eyes of the woman who laughed with him, or challenged him to yet another game of cribbage. No, these days those eyes barely met his and when they did, all warmth had vanished. Nothing but frost in her gaze these days.

"Hey, old man, you're dripping soup onto the floor." Robin continued down the hall to the two small bedrooms.

Unable to contain their curiosity, Becca and Mona came to find out what Robin was up to. From where the women stood in the hallway, they could see into both bedrooms. The tiny one had been Becca's growing up. Now the bed's springs and mattress were on their side, leaning against one wall. Cartons filled the bedroom's floor space, overflow from the storage room. The antique dresser from Becca's youth was gone, now living in Alpaca Haven on Becca's and Stan's farm, displaying handcrafted items.

The other bedroom was the one Keith and Izzy had shared. The unmade double bed took up most of the room. A small dresser doubled as Keith's bedside table. To the right of the other pillow, a TV tray stacked high with books and papers barely had room for the bedside lamp.

"What are you doing?" Keith asked as he trailed them down his hall.

The women ignored him.

"If we removed the wall between these two bedrooms, we'd have a decent-sized storage area. I bet Blair could do that in no time," Robin said to Becca and Mona.

"Hey…" Keith complained.

"Follow me," Robin told the women. Returning to the living room, she swept an arm toward the space. "Imagine this cleared out. There is lots of room for display cases and shelving. We could expand the store into here. Customers might enjoy wandering around, exploring. Maybe even run some art classes."

"I can see it! Yes!" Becca's eyes gleamed with the possibilities.

"A bit of paint, some reorganizing, and this could help the business," Mona said.

"Ladies, aren't you forgetting something? I live here," Keith protested. "This is my home. What am I supposed to do if you turn this into part of the store?"

"Move someplace else," Robin said without looking at him.

He noticed she didn't offer that he could move to her house.

Over the next few days, no one mentioned anything about expanding the store, giving Keith hope his objections made them drop the ridiculous notion.

At least no one talked about it when Keith was around. "We planted the seed," Robin told the other women. "Let's give Keith a chance to think about it."

Stan stopped by to take Becca to lunch. As soon as Becca, Mona, and Robin saw who had entered the store, they greeted the man and resumed their conversation about the store's expansion. The idea of holding art classes took root - they could tie the classes to some products for sale at Alpaca Haven, linking the two businesses even more.

"It all sounds good," Stan agreed, "but what about Keith? Where would he go? The guy has to live someplace."

"My thoughts exactly." Keith's voice came from the back of the store where he'd entered without the others being aware. "I've looked around town and there's nothing available."

"If my sister wasn't renting my house, you could have it," Mona told him.

"Thanks, but that doesn't help."

"I know what you need." This came from Robin, and for the first time in what felt like weeks, she looked directly at him. "You need one of those tiny houses. You're used to living in a small space. Those tiny houses must be cheap and quick to build. You could be in one in no time."

"Would you expect me to plant it in the back alley? I bet the town would have something to say about that. And I repeat, there are no vacant lots in town."

"Why does it have to be in town?" Stan asked. "You could build out at the farm. There's lots of room."

Keith watched as Becca's stare at her husband turned into a glare. Obviously, the two had not discussed this beforehand.

His son-in-law had not been married long; if he wanted to maintain marital bliss, he needed to heed the look Becca shot at him.

Oblivious, Stan continued. "The yard is about ten acres, so we could have two houses there and we wouldn't be in each other's hair." Turning to his wife, he asked, "Isn't that a great idea, Bec?"

Stan might be the one married to Becca, but Keith had known her far longer. She might complain that her father didn't understand her, but he knew far more about his only child than she realized. It came across loud and clear that she did not want her father living near her.

That was on him. He'd not been the most sensitive parent, and never won Father of the Year Award, hadn't even made it to the bottom of the nomination list. But he'd cared, and he'd tried, just not in ways that Becca understood or appreciated.

Things between them got worse when Becca was in high school. The girl was always mad. Or sad. Or in some kind of mood, which he never understood. He'd left Izzy to deal with the girl; he had a business to run, and besides, anything he said seemed to make things worse. All he could do was practical stuff, like keeping a roof over their heads, and ensure he had a viable business to pass on to his only offspring.

Was it all his fault, this rift between him and his daughter? Becca seemed to think so.

Without Izzy around to run interference between them, things got worse. That is, until Robin stepped in, helping him see things from the girl's perspective, and he suspected that Robin also talked to Becca about how Keith might feel.

He knew he had not been supportive enough of Becca's desire to create a farm of her own. He might have been able to get behind her if she'd wanted to get into sheep, or cattle. But alpacas? Who'd even heard of the creatures, let alone tried to make money from them?

And yet, she'd done just that. It was still in the early days, but his girl was already turning a profit. Not much of one, but the ledgers were on the positive side.

Robin told him to give it a chance, so despite his earlier objections, he drove out to Becca's and Stan's place when no one was around. He leaned on the fence, watching the little alpaca herd. Gradually the animals seemed to accept his presence, coming closer and doing this weird humming thing.

The first to approach him was Margaret. Ridiculous to name your livestock, but that is exactly what Becca did. Margaret was her favorite, and the self-proclaimed leader of the herd. She was a cute little thing, with her light fawn coat and mile-long eyelashes. The boldest of the group, Becca named her after the former British Prime Minister. When

Izzy questioned Becca on her choice of names, Becca said, "Whether or not you liked the woman, Margaret Thatcher had guts."

Although *this* Margaret never turned her ire on any person since Becca brought her home, Margaret kept her herd-mates in line with threats and sprays of spittle.

Keith smiled to himself. Sort of like Becca herself, minus the spitting.

No two of the alpacas were exactly the same hue; that was on purpose, part of Becca's plan. She wanted variety in the fleece colors, so she'd get interesting yarns without having to resort to dyes.

A dark brown one was second in command, only giving way to Margaret. This one Becca called Angela, after Angela Merkel, another gutsy European politician.

It had taken time, but Keith was a patient man. Now when he approached their fence, Margaret and Angela pushed the others out of the way to get to him first, rubbing noses, wanting a pet, and doing that humming thing. Maybe it was his unassuming stance that won them over; maybe it was that he fed them.

Whenever he was there prior to feeding time, Keith liked to do that chore for his daughter. It was a small thing and didn't take that much time. He enjoyed being outside, tending to the animals.

Maybe he had no words to express his regret over how things were between him and Becca and could not bring himself to say he was sorry, for he wasn't sure what. But he could do something practical to help his girl, especially when she wasn't looking.

He'd notice when the water system froze up one nasty winter day. Yes, he knew Stan would have taken care of it when he got home, but it would be early evening until the young man finished his own chores with the cattle on the spread he shared with his parents and brother. Keith had a water heater in the storage room at the store and all the tools. It only took a few hours that afternoon to fix, and he doubted that Becca ever knew she'd had a problem.

If he was around their place more, he could take care of things like that for them.

But not if his girl didn't want him there.

More diplomatic than Izzy or any of these women gave him credit for, Keith retreated. "Just came back to get the case of nails Beldings wanted before I take the order out to their place. I'd better be off."

Better leave than see the pity on their faces as these people realized his only child didn't want him anywhere near her home. Best let Becca save face as well.

CHAPTER 37

When Stan took her hand as they walked to the diner, Becca resisted the urge to pull away. It wasn't his fault that her father annoyed her so much, and she shouldn't take it out on Stan. But what on earth had possessed the man to offer that Dad could build a house on *their* land?

True, at one time, the farm had belonged to Keith, passed down from his parents and grandparents. But her parents signed over the land to her. Sure, she knew it was a bribe to get her to stick around, but so what? She wanted land, and now she had it.

She glanced out the side of her eye at the good-looking man beside her. Without that land, she never would have gotten reacquainted with Stan, never would have realized what an amazing guy he was, never would have fallen in love with him, and better yet, he with her.

She gave his hand a squeeze, and he flashed her that grin that always did funny things to her innards - good things, things that made her want to hum like a contented alpaca.

Still, why did he have to make that outrageous offer to her dad?

"Are you ticked with me, baby?" Stan knew her well.

"No." She had to be honest; he'd see right through her. "Sort of. Why did you suggest Dad could build on our farm?"

"It makes sense. We have the space, and he needs a place to build. You've said how excited you are about the possibility of expanding the hardware store. You can't do that the way things are now, and the guy has to live somewhere."

"True, but does he have to live near us?"

"Bec, 'near' is a relative term. If we lived in town and he was two blocks away, he'd be nearer to us than if he built a house at the other end of our farmyard."

He had a point. "But we'd run into him."

Stan's brow wrinkled. "Like you don't when you're both working at the hardware store?"

"That's different."

Stan raised an eyebrow. He held the open the door to the diner for her and followed his wife to a table.

"You're not going to tell me to give the man a chance."

"I'm not? Okay, if you say so."

"Stan," warned Becca.

He held up his hands in surrender and diverted his attention to Celeste Benson coming to take their orders.

"I know you're going to rattle off all the ways you think he's trying."

"Who, me? Nope. I wouldn't dare do that." His tone implied, "Not in the mood you're in."

"You're right. It's hard for me to look at him objectively, but he is doing some things he's never done before. He's not bugging me about taking over his store, nothing about that Feldman legacy stuff. And my alpacas like him. It's hard for me to admit that, but they do. Even Margaret, and she can be picky about who she lets pet her.

"Dad does do an okay job when he feeds them. He watches and listens to me, so he gets it right."

Stan took a chance. "He was a big help when we renovated the house, pitching in without a fuss."

"Yeah, that surprised me. He even took direction from Blair; that's a side of Dad I hadn't seen before."

"What would be so bad if he built a house on our land?"

Reid picked Mona up so they could head to her appointment with the counselor. Sometimes father and son remained in the waiting room; other times, the therapist wanted to see the wife and husband together. For those appointments, Robin and Keith kept Owen with them at the store.

Thank goodness for Owen, thought Keith. Otherwise, he and Robin would stumble around, doing useless things, doing their best to avoid each other, and he ran out of excuses for escaping her proximity.

The easy flow of conversation they had once shared now descended into stiff, meaningless social chitchat, the sort that had always left him cold. Having to keep his distance, guard every word he uttered was exhausting and so unlike the relaxed way they'd had with each other at Robin's house. Now he sought every excuse to avoid her presence.

Not that he didn't *want* to be with her; that was the problem. When it was just the two of them in a room, it was impossible to hold back images of what it had been like between them just a short month ago. The past weeks hadn't diminished the memories, the yearning to return to what they'd had, how they'd been.

What exactly had they had? They'd never talked about it, just slid into what felt comfortable, felt right.

Then he'd ruined it. All for a good cause, right? Why then did that decision churn over endlessly in his mind?

The bell over the store's front door sounded. Thank goodness. He'd accept anyone right now, friend or foe, or lost stranger.

It was neither.

"So, Dad, have you picked out a spot for your new house?"

"I told you, there are no vacant lots in town." Was the girl trying to rub it in? They'd just been over this before lunch.

"I meant a spot in our farmyard."

What? How had a short walk with her husband and some food changed Becca's attitude? Maybe he misinterpreted what she said.

"Come again, girl? What are you talking about?" Inside, he winced at the way those words came out. He had not meant to be gruff. Izzy would have given him that look, the one Robin threw his way right now. Did these women not think he could manage himself? Maybe not, from the way he kept disappointing them.

Robin jumped in. "You have only one delivery to make this afternoon, and it's out by Becca's and Stan's place."

"But..."

Robin didn't let him finish. "The snow's receding, and it's sunny, so it might be a good time for a stroll and scouting out the best location."

"I've been thinking about it," said Becca. "I like that sheltered area near where the orchard used to be. Go look at it."

What was he supposed to say? Little more than an hour

ago, his little girl looked daggers at the thought of him encroaching on her land. Now was she inviting him there? Made no sense. But this Becca was almost… friendly. Izzy would tell him to embrace it, go with the flow, and don't screw it up.

He'd try. "I remember that orchard when I was a boy. Your great-grandmother grew plums, cherries, pears, apricots, and a bunch of kinds of apples. Shame no one kept it up after she died." And why hadn't they? There never seemed to be enough time. But now? "If we could resurrect those trees, or plant new ones, you might make jams and stuff to sell in your store."

Becca rewarded him with a smile - a genuine one.

His gaze drifted of its own volition to Robin's face. She smiled, too, a fond one, the kind she used to give when he'd pleased her.

CHAPTER 38

I t was a good weekend for Robin. A busy one.
Friday and Randine came to her house after school Friday, staying until Sunday afternoon. Baking and movies and games - memory-making times with her foster granddaughters.

As fun as it had been, relief registered in a tiny part of Robin's brain as she drove the girls back home. Wonderful as the kids were, their energy wore her down.

Nothing against Friday or Randine; they were simply kids, and she was an old woman, used to being on her own. She loved her little house, and the solitude it provided. Being alone wasn't the same as being lonely.

Or so she told herself.

Funny. When she first moved into town, she'd felt only contentment. She loved her son, but it felt right to move out of the farmhouse they shared, the one where she'd spent most of her adult life, the one with all the memories of Ron.

She and Ron may not have started out as the perfect love match, at least on her part. They'd dated in high school, but while Ron wanted nothing but to farm in Goodrich County, nineteen-year-old Robin's heart wanted more. All she'd ever known was the rural area of Goodrich. Could she truly settle down there without seeing what else the world offered?

She'd known she wounded Ron when she left for the city with another man. Boy, really. But something inside her compelled her to go, to explore what was out there, to experience other ways of living.

She had found those other ways. Rather than acres of free space to roam, they'd rented a cramped, damp basement apartment. She had to tilt her head to glimpse the sun and sky through the narrow windows near the ceiling, seeking the nature scenes she'd taken for granted her whole life.

Starting her new life, she escaped the endless chores of farm life, replacing them with minimum wage jobs as a store clerk or waitress. Even though the latter was harder work, at least the tips brought in a bit more money.

Never had she given a thought to food - it was just there. She, along with her sisters, griped about how much they had to help in the garden, but now the price of those same vegetables in the supermarket astounded her. Even worse, they didn't taste as good - they just didn't.

Growing up, everyone had to help with chores to do with the livestock, haying and harvesting grain. Didn't matter that they weren't boys; her dad taught his three daughters to run the tractors, change oil, grease and lube the equipment, and spend long hours in the field. Glamorous? No way.

Then again, neither was waitressing. Life beyond Goodrich wasn't the utopia she'd imagined.

Dreams of her romantic life in the city cracked when she discovered she was pregnant, then shattered when her boyfriend ran out on her. Becoming a father played no part in his plans.

Without him sharing expenses with her, she could no longer afford the apartment. A second job seemed the answer, but either the long hours stressed her pregnancy, or the pregnancy made her too sick and exhausted to keep this up.

With one tearful phone call, her parents arrived, packed her up, and welcomed her back home. Within days of her return, Ron showed up, hesitant, but that steely determination of his showed he would do whatever it took to win her back.

Impossible to be anything but honest with this good man, Robin told him about her pregnancy. At first she thought the ice in his eyes was meant for her, but his words told her what he'd do to the man who abandoned her if he ever showed his face around here again.

Ron had only one stipulation - two, really. That they marry right away, and that they raise the child as his own. No one else was to know that the baby was not his. She'd kept that promise, right until a year ago when she shared the secret with Blair.

They'd made a good life together, she and Ron. She'd always known he loved her. On her part, fondness and caring and proximity grew into love.

She could still remember the panic of his first heart attack. But he wasn't old, and lots of people had heart attacks, then lived full lives for decades longer. She and Ron were healthy people who ate well and got plenty of exercise and fresh air. This heart stuff was a temporary blip.

Until the second one. That one they both took more seriously, altering their diet, reducing the size of their cattle herd, and taking things easier.

It hadn't worked. His death tore out her own heart. How to explain to someone else the visceral pain, the blade that struck deep and kept on slashing away chunks of her?

She'd lost her parents, one at a time. She'd been through the agony of her sister's and brother-in-law's deaths in that car accident. All painful, but those things didn't touch the depth of torture of losing her husband.

Coming back from that had not been easy and there'd been many, many dark days when the shadows never lifted. Slowly, glimmers of light penetrated the clouds some days, then more and more days. The pain would never go away; she'd lost an enormous chunk of herself when he died.

But she'd learned to live again. She had her sister and Phoebe's family. She had her son, and now her son's family. The girls sitting in the back seat of her car were a bonus.

They'd had a good time this weekend, the three of them. Although she'd relish the quiet of having her home to herself again, a tiny part of her brain questioned if it would be too silent.

Why? She'd always been a quiet kind of gal, with no need for noise and crowds around her. She liked her little house, she truly did.

The best times in that house, though, had been those she shared with Keith.

CHAPTER 39

R obin's and Beth's eyes met. The kitchen filled with
the girls' chatter, each one vying to tell Beth about
their weekend. That was fine; Friday and Randine
would wind down, then Robin and Beth would have time to
chat. She enjoyed spending time with the woman Blair chose
for his wife.

Robin noticed the table set for eight, not five. "Am I not
your only guest for supper tonight?"

"I forgot to tell you. Becca and Stan and Keith are
coming."

Keith. Why did even his name make her insides fluttery?
Must be that she had just been thinking of him.

She was a grown woman, not a schoolgirl with a crush.
Get over it, she told herself. You work for the man. Their
families were tied in ways that meant they'd see each often.
So, they'd had a… what? An interlude? An affair? An
innocent one, to be sure, but why had it felt so good?

A fanciful, lonely old woman was what she was. She
needed to keep busy, to be more involved with the other

people in her life. Take this weekend, for example - she'd been too busy for thoughts of Keith to enter her head.

Liar.

Robin brought herself back to the present, to what Beth was saying. The younger woman faced the stove and seemed to not notice that her mother-in-law had drifted off. She caught Beth's words mid-sentence.

"... blueprints. Tiny homes vary quite a bit. We can build them on a foundation or on wheels, meant to be pulled down a road. Keith's insisting on the latter." She gave Robin a rueful smile. "It's almost like he doesn't trust he and Becca will get along in the same yard, and fears he'll be sent on his way."

Yeah, that sounded like Keith, preparing for the worst. "How big are tiny homes? I've only seen pictures of them."

"To meet regulations for highway transport, most are about 8 1/2 feet wide, 13 1/2 feet high, and between 20 and 28 feet long."

"Twenty-eight feet doesn't sound bad. That's the width of some houses."

"True, but the width means that most tiny homes have only around 200 square feet on the main floor."

"Are they two-storey then?"

"Can be, although most have only a partial second floor; the openness of a higher ceiling dispels some of the cramped feeling. But with the height's outer dimension of only 13 1/2 feet, the two-storey part has either only six-foot ceilings, or regular height on the first floor, and only five feet upstairs."

"Even I'd have to stoop at that height."

"Depending on how much Keith wants to spend, there are some movable tiny homes built on a gooseneck trailer that are longer, and placing the bedroom over the gooseneck part means the walls can be a normal height."

"That sounds better."

"Blair wonders how it would do in our winters, though. He likes things sturdy, and prefers a solid frame built into the ground for insulation."

"Hmm. Wonder how this is going to work," said Robin. "In my experience, Blair usually gets things his way. But Keith is the most stubborn man I've come across."

"More so than Blair?"

"You'd better believe it. Once he gets a notion in his head, there is no changing him, no matter how unreasonable it is."

B lair had been looking forward to this meeting. Challenges intrigued him; since his return to farming, he'd not had as much time as he'd like to work on carpentry projects.

Building a tiny home intrigued him; building one *with* Keith less so, although the man had been nothing but helpful those times he'd dropped in to work on Stan's and Becca's farmhouse renovations. The guy had skills, so it wasn't like working with a newbie apprentice, and he'd followed instructions without complaint.

The real stickler to this evening was his mother. Not that he had anything against her, but this was the first time since Christmas that they'd had both her and Keith over at the same time. That dinner still galled him, the possessive way the man had put his arm across the back of his mother's chair. Beth telling him to mind his own business or to get over it did nothing to help. Nor did her laughing at his concerns.

He'd watch carefully tonight.

.   .   .

K eith arrived with Stan and Becca since he'd been at
their place, surveying possible house sites with them.
At least Becca and her dad didn't seem to argue about where
the house might go, thank goodness. Although Keith was on
the grouchy side on his good days, Becca never backed down
from anything, especially with her father. Stan's good nature
worked as a go-between the two of them, something Blair
knew he could never do.

He needn't have worried about his mom today. She
greeted Becca and her nephew, Stan, with hugs, but only
nodded at Keith.

The older man hung back. "I thought we were just
meeting with Blair and Beth. I didn't know you'd be here,
too, Robin."

His mother snapped at the man. "This is *my* son's home,
and my daughter-in-law invited me for supper."

Good, thought Blair, watching Keith retreat to the other
side of the room, not glancing again at Robin.

S upper was a noisy meal with eight of them around the
table, multiple conversations going on at once, almost
everyone boisterous. Except Keith. And Robin. His mother
was unusually quiet. Maybe the girls had worn her out this
weekend. Goodness knows *he* was weary, just listening to
them chatter about all they'd done with his mom.

CHAPTER 40

With the dishes cleared away, and the girls in the other room, the six adults gathered around the table.

Based on the features Keith said he wanted in a place, Beth brought out some tiny home designs she'd found, ones built onto a trailer, ready to be moved.

Blair held his tongue while Keith looked them over.

"Any of these would do. I'm not picky."

Becca and Blair exchanged glances. Who was Keith kidding?

Glancing at her husband for the go-ahead, Beth explained some of her misgivings about the layouts they'd discussed before. "Most of these designs have a loft bedroom. To save space, some use ladders to get to the loft." She left that hang.

"Dad, aren't you a little old to be scaling ladders to get to bed?" Becca asked.

They all noticed Keith stiffen. Couldn't Becca have phrased that a bit more delicately?

"You're right. I don't fancy climbing ladders, especially with my hip."

Robin interrupted. "It looks like these have bathrooms on the main floor."

"That's right."

"A ladder would never work for someone who has to get up several times in the night to use the bathroom."

Blair glared at his mother. "How would *you* know how many times Keith gets up in the night?"

"I lived with your father for 40 years. Things change as you get older and your bladder capacity shrinks. I don't know of anyone of 60, or even 50, who hasn't found that to be true. It would be better if the toilet was on the same floor as the bedroom."

Blair backed down.

Beth continued. "Since the height of these mobile tiny houses is restricted to 13.5 feet if they are to be towed down the highway, the upstairs often has a mattress on the floor and only a five or six-foot ceiling."

"You mean I'd have to crawl into bed? Or spend my life stooped over?"

"If you stuck to this type of design, yes."

"How am I going to get up in the morning if I'm practically sleeping on the floor?"

"Space is an issue, no matter how cleverly storage is designed. They build these trailers to hold a house between 20 and 28 feet long. A 20 by 8.5 foot house gives you only 170 square feet of living space. That's only slightly larger than this kitchen."

They all looked around at the space filled with bodies and furniture and stacked dishes.

"Not much room for a bathroom, or a place to watch TV," admitted Keith.

"There's another type of trailer used for a base," Beth said. "A gooseneck trailer. By building the bedroom over the gooseneck, there are only a few steps to climb, and there can be enough headroom for you to stand up."

"That sounds better. Let's go with that."

Blair's turn. "I have some concerns about that option. It would be fine in the summer, and maybe even in spring and fall, but imagine the icy wind sweeping under the gooseneck area in the winter."

"Good point." Keith could see that. "But wouldn't that be true of anything built on a trailer?"

"Yes. We could erect an insulated frame around the whole thing, but the cost might be just as much as building a permanent structure."

"But I need to be able to move the house if I have to."

"Why?" asked Stan.

"Yeah, why," Becca echoed. "Are you planning on leaving us soon?"

"Well, no, but it seems like a sensible precaution, just in case."

"In case of what?" Becca's voice rose, her eyes narrowing.

Stan defused things. "Here's the thing, Keith. This house will be an asset on the property. If you ever decided you wanted to move away, we could buy the building from you.

"On the other hand, you'll likely stay. With you living nearby, one day when we have kids, they'll be close to their grandfather. You already help with the alpacas sometimes - not that I want to eat up your spare time, but there are days when we could really use your help around the place."

With things headed in this direction, Blair added his piece. "The house would be much better insulated if I set it into the ground. Whether you decide on a full basement, or just a crawl space, doesn't matter. But warmth under your floors will make a big difference to your heating bill and to your comfort."

Beth pulled out a folder of other plans. "If you're set on a tiny house, here are some layouts for 16 by 30 foot, and 20 by 30-foot homes. The latter would give you 600 square feet of space. You can do a lot with that instead of under 200 or 300 feet. Without the trailer restrictions, it can be two-storey, giving you all the room you'd need." She arranged some papers on the table, showing exterior and interior shots.

Keith picked up the first one.

Robin rose from her chair. Resting one hand on Keith's shoulder, she leaned forward to get a better look.

No one but Keith and Blair noticed.

Blair watched as Keith became unfocused on the drawings in front of him, and one of the man's hands rose as if to cover Robin's with his own. He seemed to catch himself and pretended to scratch his nose instead.

Blair studied his mom. She seemed unaware of how familiarly she had touched that man. Why would she feel free to touch him? Blair wouldn't have done that to any woman but his wife. It wasn't like Robin had a problem with her balance. And she kept her hand there.

"Oh, no," said Robin. "This won't work."

Everyone except Keith looked at her.

"Why not?" Blair asked.

"Look at that kitchen! It's way too small."

"Mom, it's called a *tiny* house for a reason. And I doubt Keith spends his days cooking up feasts."

"Of course not, but how could I ever do anything decent in a kitchen like that?"

Silence.

Keith's eyes remained glued to the table, his back rigid.

Blair and Beth exchanged glances. Beth's look warned him to be gentle.

He tried. "Mom, I thought this was *Keith's* house we're talking about."

Was that a blush on his mother's face? Nothing usually fazed her.

"I know that!" Robin didn't meet anyone's gaze. "But this house will be on Becca's land, and she has a store to stock. There will be garden and orchard produce to prepare if we're going to sell preserves and jellies. Becca's kitchen will be full. It makes no sense for me to cart produce all the way back to town for me to work on. If there are two kitchens on the farm, then both should be used for the benefit of the store."

Now Keith did pat the hand that still inexplicably remained on his shoulder. "You and Becca are most welcome to use any kitchen space I have."

Blair eyed the couple. Was there more behind those words?

CHAPTER 41

In the end, it was Beth and Robin who chose the
ultimate design for Keith's new house, a house that
would sit on a foundation, not a movable trailer. As a
former interior designer Beth, had the skills to bring Robin's
ideas to life. Blair, with his knowledge of carpentry and
codes, made sure everything would be sound.

Keith went along with whatever the other three
suggested.

With one exception. He waited until no one was around
but Blair. All his life, he'd fallen in with what others expected
of him. It felt odd, even selfish, to want something just for
himself now.

Blair was a craftsman, so maybe he'd understand. How to
broach this?

"If I'm moving out of the store, there are a lot of things I'll
need to take with me."

"Yeah," said Blair. Was that not obvious?

"I've been admiring things you've made for Alpaca Haven.
The carvings and the toys are well done. Exceptional."

Blair was not used to compliments from the older man

and wasn't sure he'd ever heard Keith compliment anyone. "Thanks. I only wish I had more time to work on them. Or better tools."

"Tools. That's what I wanted to talk to you about."

"Don't worry, I have all the equipment necessary to build your house."

"That's not what I'm talking about." How to ease into this? "Where do you do your woodworking?"

"In the barn. Now that I'm reducing my cattle herd, I don't need the barn for birthing cows, or ones I need to keep quarantined. Except for Clarabelle, of course. Mom would kill me if I ever talked about getting rid of her."

"I've tasted Clarabelle's offerings, and I think Robin is right." Would it be too nosy to ask? "I'd like to see your space sometime, if I might."

"You would? It's just a barn, but it no longer holds equipment or hay. There's a decent amount of room when you don't have to contend with cattle. I've only started renovating it, but it has potential."

"Could I take a look?"

Beth and Robin were fussing about some of the house's interior storage details. They'd needed Keith's approval on a couple of points; that's why he'd driven out, but he cared little about the smaller stuff.

Pulling on their boots and coats, the two men followed the path the snowblower made from the house to the barn.

The entry part of the barn, and Clarabelle's stall, remained much the way they always had. But a door led them into the renovated part. Freshly wired, insulated, dry walled and painted, the place smelled new. Shelving and cabinets and workstations lined the walls. In the center sat an 8- by 8-foot platform holding a table saw. A router and its case sat on the bench.

"Do you have a stand for that router?" Keith asked.

"I wish. Maybe one day."

"I have one. I bought it, and a router and accessories a few years ago. Somehow, I thought I'd find the space and time to use it. Neither happened." He hesitated. "If you'd like, I could bring it out and set it up here."

"You mean store it here?"

"I mean, keep it here for you to use, and maybe for me to use sometimes, too." Then he added, "If that would be okay with you."

"Of course."

"I also have a scroll saw and a band saw, all still in their cases, never used."

Blair looked at the guy.

"I know. I somehow had the idea I could get into woodworking, but the time was never right." He added, "And two lathes, as well."

"Man, what don't you have?"

"A table saw."

"Know how to use one?"

"Other than the basics, I'm better on the theory than the doing. Lack of opportunity, but I've read woodworking magazines and watched lots of YouTube videos."

Blair grinned. "How did we learn things before YouTube?" He thought about this. "So you're saying you'd like to work with wood, and you'd share your tools with me, and I'd share my space?"

"I think they'd become *our* tools. And you probably have some things I don't, that I might want to use."

"What would you make?"

"Things for Becca to sell in her store."

Blair held out his hand. "Keith, my man, I think we have a deal."

Keith shook. "There are a couple of other things I'd like to get straight, first. One, I know you have your own stuff to do and taking on a house is an extensive project. I don't want you to feel pressure that you have to build this for me. I can hire someone else if you'd prefer or buy one ready-made and have it moved here."

"What? A ready-made one wouldn't have all the details Mom and Beth seem to think so important for your house."

"True, but they'd have to get over it."

"Hmm." He doubted that. "It will cost you a lot more to purchase a pre-built. And I can guarantee that they won't build it as well as I could for you."

"Son, I don't doubt that at all. I just didn't want you to feel that you had to take on this job. But, if you do, I'd rather pay you to do it than give the money to some stranger."

"Appreciate that, Keith. I'm still working out the costs, but we'll do it as economically as possible. With Stan, Reid, and Greg helping, it shouldn't take long to put up a 600 square foot building."

"And me. I'll do my share of the labor."

"Deal. Now, we'd better get back to the house before those women add in anything else."

"Ah, there is one more thing I'd like to add. I'd like a garage."

"That shouldn't be a problem."

"I mean, a garage that I wouldn't use to store my truck. There are two hobbies I've wanted to take up. One is woodworking, and the other is welding. I'd like a welding shop."

"Talk to Stan. He's the welding guy."

"I don't mean the kind of welding Stan does, like that grand sign for Becca's alpacas." Keith had trouble meeting Blair's eyes. Would he think him a fanciful old man? "I'd like to weld junk. You know, backyard craft junk. Have you seen those things?"

"Yeah, I have. They're hot sellers at craft fairs. You'd want to put them in Becca's store?"

Keith nodded.

"They'd fit in well." Blair thought about it. "A double garage would give you plenty of room for the larger pieces you'd want to weld. We'd need to put in 240 wiring to give you options, and a ventilation system, but that's all doable. I can see one problem, though."

"What's that?"

"You're going to have Stan hanging out at your place."

"If he gets too annoying, I'll come over here and calm myself by doing something with wood."

While they were having a decent conversation, Blair had something else to say. "I need to apologize to you for my mother. She's taking over this project, almost as if it's her house. I've tried to shut her down, but you know Mom."

"It's fine. I don't have many ideas for inside the house, so we can leave that to your wife and mother. Robin knows what suits me."

CHAPTER 42

B eing alone every evening gave Keith time for reflection - too much time. He tried to block out thoughts he didn't want to have by learning new things. YouTube videos were a substantial source of information as long as you could tell the crack pots from those who knew what they were talking about. Although the women who worked in his store believed him a Luddite with technology, he was better than they knew. Why would he disabuse them of their notions?

Tonight was a bad night. Women. None of what he found on the screen kept his mind from the women in his life.

Robin. Nope, he would not allow his mind to wander in that direction. Nor his heart. Maybe their present state was all for the best. He'd enjoyed his time with her, perhaps too much.

He'd made one woman the center of his universe. The pain of losing her nearly destroyed him, and no way could he survive a loss like that again. He'd been right in shutting things down with Robin before they got too far. Why would he risk letting another woman become close? Better to be alone than chance ever falling into that world of hurt again.

Izzy was not far from his thoughts; she probably would always be there, taking up a sizeable chunk of his heart. But she'd be ticked with him if all he did was mope around, wishing she were still there. His Izzy was practical and believed in getting on with things. That's what she'd tell him to do now.

And to make things right with their girl.

He was trying. It wasn't easy to change a lifetime of habitual ways of interacting. This paying attention to the feelings of others was a pain. Who had the time or the inclination to constantly try to put yourself in someone else's shoes? He used to have Izzy to do such things for him, only pestering him about it when it really mattered.

For a while there, Robin had taken on that roll, helping smooth out the abrasive edges of his interactions with his daughter. It worked, too. He and Becca could be in the same room now without automatically butting heads. His girl had mellowed. Maybe it was married life that did it, or maybe following her dream of an alpaca farm. Whatever it was, she was easier to get along with.

Robin had told him that might be because *he* changed. He'd stopped forcing his daughter to conform to the box he'd decided was the best way for her to live her life. His efforts were pointless, anyway; Becca never listened to him.

Funny, but that's a complaint Izzy made about him, especially where Becca was concerned. She warned him that he would drive the girl away if he didn't stop pressuring her. Izzy was right; their daughter ran clear across the ocean to get away from this town and his expectations of her.

Was this such an awful place to live? And was running a successful business in town so horrid?

To Becca, it was. When she fled Goodrich County, he'd

been bitter over how little sense of duty the child had. There was a responsibility in being the third generations of Feldman's running the hardware store. Honor. Tradition. Yet Becca felt none of those things, willing to toss it all away.

But she was home. Settled permanently in the area. He had Stan and the alpacas to thank for that.

Although Izzy had kept their books, Keith wasn't bad with finances. He'd had to learn when his father passed away, leaving the store in precarious shape. It had taken years to get the place on a firm financial footing. While not wealthy, he was comfortable, as long as he did nothing foolish.

He and Izzy each had life insurance policies - the bank required them for some loans they'd needed over the years. Once the loans were paid off, they'd continued with the policies at Izzy's insistence. They were each other's beneficiaries and when Izzy died, the money came to him.

He immediately gave half to Becca. Their daughter assumed Izzy named her co-beneficiary with her dad; Keith never told her otherwise. Becca and Stan would never finish their house renovations if they had to rely on money from their salaries to pay for materials. Becca didn't make a fortune from the part-time hours she put in at the hardware store and Stan, well he was a hard worker and good man, but the money he brought in depended on cattle and grain prices, things out of his control, and his farm had expenses.

The life insurance money allowed the couple to purchase the supplies they needed, and even hire some workers to help speed up the project. Besides, with Becca's alpaca business in its infancy, she needed extra capital to see her through the start-up pains.

Izzy would approve of what he'd done with her life

insurance money, even with investing in his new house so the girls could expand the hardware store.

He crunched numbers some more, just to be certain he had things right. Meetings with an accountant, a lawyer and bank loans officer completed, he was fairly confident in his decision. Now, if the girls cooperated…

~

"Ladies, I need to talk to you about something." Keith turned the 'Open' sign to 'Closed' and locked the store's front door. From the back room, he brought out a box of donuts, a carafe of freshly brewed coffee, and four mugs. He needed to do this right.

"I have a proposition for you."

"Dad, I am *not* taking over the store."

"Young lady, I am aware of your feelings on this topic. You've made yourself clear."

"Yeah, but did you listen?" mumbled Becca.

"Yes." He would not argue; this was too important.

He had Mona's, Becca's and Robin's full attention now. "I'd like to retire, or semi-retire. Spend more time doing the things I always wanted to do and spend less time here at the store."

He could see the worry in Mona's eyes. Her salary meant a lot to her and Reid. Did she think he was shutting down the store? That girl worried too much. Hopefully, what he offered would help.

"I had this business appraised."

"Dad, are you planning to sell?" Becca asked.

"Girl, let me tell this in my own way." Where did she get that impatience from? Izzy had never been like that. "I've seen an accountant and a lawyer. I want to incorporate this business.

"My plan is that there would be four shareholders, each owing an equal part, with equal say." He held up his hand to stop Becca as she opened her mouth. "I'd like the joint owners to be the four of us in this room."

The women looked at him as if they couldn't understand his words. Wasn't it obvious? "I admit I've been stuck in my old ways. The three of you have fresh ideas for this business, good ones, despite what I might have said originally. You work well together and will make your mark here.

"Originally, we'd planned on passing this store on to Becca." He watched her face. "I know, I know, girl. That is not what you want. My plan, my *new* plan, is for Becca and I to jointly keep half of the business, while the two of you would own the other half."

"But…" The worry in Mona's eyes deepened.

"I've talked to the bank. Mona and Robin, if you're interested, your quarter ownership in Feldman's Hardware will mean a buy-in that is doable."

"I can't, we can't afford…" tried Mona.

"Hear me out, girlie. This business is doing better with all your ideas. It can afford to give dividends to the four owners." His gaze took in all of them. "The three of you would continue to receive your salaries as you do now. In addition, you'd each get a monthly dividend from the company, a dividend that would cover your loan payment." He'd already cleared it with the bank that his dividends would go to help pay down Mona and Robin's loans.

"Think about it, ladies. There is very little risk for you, and income to be made. Robin, give it a few days, and discuss it with your son."

Robin's chin jutted out, and her mouth opened.

"I know what you're going to say. He's your son, not your boss, but he's also a businessman, and it doesn't hurt to consider his opinion." He turned to Mona. "Talk about it with your husband. If he wants to see the books, I'm fine with that. The three of you already have access to our bookkeeping."

Keith unlocked the front door and flipped to sign to 'Open'. "I have deliveries to make, so I'll leave you to it."

lair surveyed the structure. Pleased with the finished product, the house was almost ready to move in, his part done. Beth insisted there were finishing touches to work on - Beth, along with Robin.

How had his mother wormed her way into this project? It was almost like it was *Robin's* house. She had more say in how things looked than did Beth, the interior designer, and definitely more say than Keith.

That man seemed content to let Robin have her way. His mother could be a force, he knew, but how did she have so much sway over someone who wasn't even family?

"I have a hard time believing some of these touches are for Keith's benefit," Blair complained to Beth.

"Some of them are things a woman would look for in a home."

"Is she projecting her wishes onto Keith's house? Do you think she's unhappy with her place in town and wants us to build her a place of her own here on the farm too?"

Beth got that look that told him he was dense. She wasn't lying, but she wasn't telling him everything she knew. Or suspected. "No, I've never gotten that sense from her. I think it's *Keith's* place that holds her interest."

"Why?"

"That's something you should ask your mother."

Robin was sick of it - those looks from her son. True, Beth watched her, too, but without censure, just curiosity. Annoying, yes, but not in the way Blair irritated her.

What right did he have to watch her and Keith? Judge her? So what if she helped with the man's new house? Getting Keith's place in order meant spending time with him. *That* was none of her son's business.

For most of her life, she'd played peacemaker. Growing up with her sisters, she'd been the go-between, settling disputes, and keeping things calm in their household. Once married, her role was mediator between her husband and son.

Ron believed he was doing right by Blair, raising him to be nothing like his biological father. Blair turned into a responsible young man with skills and a chip on his shoulder, who felt nothing but criticism from the man who brought him up. Ron could be exacting, but he'd been proud of their son, just never let Blair know that.

Sometimes keeping peace in their home exhausted her.

Now, Ron was gone, and Blair back in the farmhouse with his wife and foster daughters. Maintaining peace in the house was up to them. Robin was done.

This was her seventh decade. Enough mediating for everyone. It was her turn to do what she liked, what felt right for her.

For a while, Keith had felt right with her, until he messed

it up. The old Robin would have placated him, done something to maintain the status quo, to make sure he was all right.

But not the new and improved Robin. Nope, he could go his way and do whatever he wanted. She would please herself.

Except she hadn't felt pleased. She'd missed the old coot and the times they'd spent together in her house, just the two of them. Those had been good times, times she hadn't thought she'd ever have again - that easy companionship with a man who demanded nothing of her, other than being herself. With him, she *had* been able to please herself. Sure, she'd done things for him, but he'd done things for her, too, things without being asked.

They'd been good together, almost like a second chance at happiness, at a life with someone.

Until he'd ruined it.

Maybe he backed away for the reasons he'd said, fear of coming between her and her son. As if that even made sense. What business was it of Blair's who she spent time with?

But maybe Keith used that as an excuse, and he ran, scared of the closeness developing between them. She'd felt it, too, that tremor of fear. Having lost someone already, she knew the pain she risked if she got close to someone, and it happened again.

Part of Robin's solution to loneliness had always been to keep busy. Learn a new hobby, take on a project, do something for someone else.

When Keith embarked on his tiny house project, it was only natural that she get involved. After all, it had been her idea for him to move out of his apartment behind the store.

Plus, she knew the man well, and he would be useless at decorating, let alone knowing the details that would make his house a home.

So what if that meant spending more time in the man's presence? She could deal. She was an adult who could do what she pleased.

Keith never seemed to mind. Blair did, but who cared what he thought?

Over the months, she and Keith had once again become easy with one another, enjoying each other's company. That feeling of companionship returned. Nothing wrong with being close to someone.

But was she risking her heart?

CHAPTER 44

They'd chosen a soft gray for the walls, white trim, darker gray planks for the flooring, and medium gray leather furniture. That is, Robin and Beth chose the colors, and everything else.

Keith sank into the cushions now, watching the crackling flames. He'd never had a fireplace before but got the appeal. The air-tight fireplace nestled beneath the television hung over the mantle. It was late spring, and perhaps a fire was unnecessary, but it was nice. So much about this was. He glanced at his companion.

Beside him, Robin sat swirling the merlot in her glass.

He'd only moved in two weeks ago. During that time, Robin had dropped in almost every day. At first, it was to add some finishing touch to the decor, or to check how an appliance worked. The first few times, she'd popped in and out, but it seemed churlish not to invite her to linger, especially when the woman had devoted so much time to making this place feel like a home.

And it did; more so than anyplace he had ever lived before. It showed when an interior designer had a hand in the planning. It also showed when a woman who knew him well did the decorating.

The place reminded him of Robin's house in town, the calm the colors and layout brought. No clutter. No piles. Yet space for all the things that mattered to him.

Including the woman beside him. Yes, she mattered.

As the house build progressed, they'd spent more and more time together. Maybe the proximity, or maybe they'd moved on, but whatever the reason, even their hours together at the hardware store had gotten easier. The wariness between them lessened, bringing them back to how things had been earlier in the winter.

Since moving into his new house, he and Robin slipped into their old ways, except this time it was Robin coming to *his* house, rather than him spending all his spare time as hers.

It felt right. It made him happy. Was that the right word to describe this feeling?

He was so not good with this feeling stuff. Izzy would have named it for him. Sometimes lately, he sensed maybe she was, and that she approved.

Becca, and sometimes even Izzy, had accused him of being oblivious to the feelings of others. When he noticed, what was the point of mentioning anything when bringing it up might cause turmoil? Letting things be was the safer course, with less risk of getting embroiled in things better avoided. Personal stuff came with messy emotions, something to be avoided at all costs.

But Robin wasn't her usual sunny self right now, giving her glass of wine far more attention than it warranted. She'd been good to him; the least he could do was reciprocate.

"Are you okay?" he asked.

"I'm fine."

How did he know she'd say that? He'd chosen the wrong

words. Try again. "Something seems to be bothering you." He hoped it wasn't him.

Still staring into her wine, it took Robin a few seconds to reply. "It's Blair."

"Is he all right?"

"Physically, yes, but it bugs me the way he watches me, as if he has the right to poke his nose into my life."

"He's your son. He has a right to be interested in your life."

"Are you going to start *that* again?"

No way. He did not want to be the recipient of her glare. "What makes you think he's watching you?"

"He is whenever I'm near you."

Uh oh. The last time Blair disapproved of his involvement with Robin, Keith had walked away.

This time would be different; they'd talk about it, no matter how much his instinct told him to run. "He doesn't like you spending time with me." This was more a statement than a question.

"It's none of his business."

Saying 'true', or 'you are his business' could both get him in trouble. There had to be something more neutral. "I think he and I understand each other more now." He grinned to ease the situation. "We bonded over woodworking."

Robin's shoulders lowered just slightly. "He's thrilled that you brought over your tools to add to his. And he welcomes you into his space in the barn; he wouldn't do that to just anyone."

"I like your son; he's a good man."

"Yes, he is, but he takes this protection thing too far."

"Is it me he objects to, or would it be any man he thinks his mother is interested in?"

Robin shot him a quick look. "Is that what you think this is?"

It was now or never. He could almost feel Izzy prodding him on, telling him to man up, and not run from this. "Or maybe he's leery of me being interested in his mother."

"Are you?"

"Yes. Very." There, he'd said it.

"How interested?"

The woman would not make this easy. "I like what we have; I liked how things were between us, those times we spent at your house."

Robin waited.

He took a sip of his wine, the words Dutch courage running through his brain. "It was comfortable."

She said nothing.

"It was easy." Oops, from her scowl, that was not the right thing to say. "What I mean to say is that I'm not good with people. I usually prefer to spend time by myself. But with you, I don't want to run away and hide. I just want to be with you."

"I enjoy being with you, too."

He'd dodged a bullet there, but making it through this minefield would be tricky. The instinct to withdraw reared its head, so easy to do, so entrenched in his way of being. Yet, the possibilities of this new way of being held even more appeal. Was it worth the risk?

There was no fool like an old fool. "I appreciate all you've done here. You've made my move easier than I thought possible." One corner of his mouth rose. "You may have noticed I can be set in my ways."

"Oh yeah, I've noticed."

"This new house is nice. Really nice. But it is less nice when you go home at night. It's like the best part of the place is missing."

Robin blinked rapidly several times.

Couldn't the woman say anything? Why was she making

him do it all? He turned, taking one of her hands in his. "Robin, I had a good thing with Izzy. I'll always miss her, but she's gone, and I never thought I'd want to be with another woman again."

Robin put her wineglass onto the coffee table, beside the coaster not on it. Her eyes never left Keith's.

"We've known each other a long time, were friends as couples. Those parts of our lives are no more. For a while after Izzy's death, it felt like my life was over, too, but it wasn't. I'm still here, and while Izzy will always own a corner of me, it seems my heart has room for more.

"You, Robin Windstrom, have wormed your way in."

"Is that a good thing?"

"From my point of view, a *very* good thing. I want you there." He gestured around the room. "I want you here." There, he'd said it. He couldn't put his heart on the line any more than that.

"I love you, too."

"What?" What had the woman said?

Robin's smile lit up the room and all the shadows that remained in his soul. "I said that I love you, too."

Gutsy woman. "How did you know I love you?"

"I know you, Keith Feldman, and in your bumbling way, that was what you were trying to say. Am I right?"

"You're right, so right." Reaching for her, he folded Robin in his arms. Her head found the perfect resting place on his shoulder. Life was too short. Not trusting someone was bad; it cut you off from good people, from a richer life. He'd taken a risk, and it paid off.

"Robin, would you do me the honor of marrying me?"

How would you like a front row seat at Robin and Keith's

wedding? Help yourself to this bonus three chapter epilogue and see how their special day turns out.
Download your copy here: https://BookHip.com/NQSGCNC

Would you like a **free** story?

Download *In Case of Rain* here: https://BookHip.com/XMSWXWN

In Case of Rain

A love for all seasons.
A chance meeting spurred by curiosity.
Avoiding the dreaded family reunion, Beth followed her impulse.
Samuel never expected the perfect woman to drop into his tractor cab.
A love he never knew he'd been looking for.

Read this short story, part of **The Farmers of Goodrich County** series.

If you enjoyed *The Farmer's Second Chance*, the author would be most appreciative if you would leave a review where you purchased the book. It need not be long, just a star rating (5 *s means you loved it!), and a few short sentences.

Want to read more about Mona and Reid?

Follow them, and their friends, Becca and Stan in
The Farmer Says I Do

Becca had vowed never to return to the small town where she grew up. Now, guess where she was? With her father's injury, there was no choice but to go home to help out.

Stan lived for farming, proud of his accomplishments, content with his life. That is, until Becca returned and stole land right out from under him. Land he used to feed his cattle.

Now she needs his help.

How could they possibly work together, especially with the push/pull chemistry flowing between them?

Read *The Farmer Says I Do*, book 2 of the Farmers of Goodrich County series of clean and wholesome romances.

The Farmer's Christmas Duty
Book 3 of the Farmers of Goodrich County series of clean and wholesome romances.
Beth is the school counselor, devoted to the well-being of her students.
Blair had good reason to distrust therapists. Just leave him alone to manage his farm.
They rubbed each other the wrong way. But now, the students need them, and for the good of the community, they must work together.

This is *so* not going well.

Read this enemies-to-lovers clean and wholesome Christmas romance.

The Farmer's Second Chance - A Later-in-Life Romance

Book 4 of the Farmers of Goodrich County series.

Robin might have lost her husband five years ago, but that didn't mean *her* life was over.
Different, yes, but different didn't have to mean bad. Maybe it was time to try new things.

Keith hated new. Stick with the tried and true, what worked now, and for his father before him. When his wife, Izzy, had been alive, they'd managed just fine.

His daughter and his employees were ganging up on him, refusing to leave things be. What was with these pesky women trying to change things?

Especially Robin.
Why did he feel compelled to listen to her? To *be* with her?

ALSO BY SHARON A. MITCHELL

Farmers of Goodrich County Series:

The Farmer Takes a Wife

The Farmer Says I Do

The Farmer's Christmas Duty

The Farmer's Second Chance - a Later-in-Life Romance

In Case of Rain (free short story)

Psychological Thrillers:

Gone: A Psychological Thriller Book 1

Trust: A Psychological Thriller Book 2

Selfish: A Psychological Thriller Book 3

Instinct: A Psychological Thriller Book 4

Reasons Why: A Psychological Thriller Book 5

Mine: A Psychological Thriller Book 6

Sanctum: A Psychological Thriller Book 7

When Bad Things Happen Box Set - Books 1 - 3

Young Anna (**free short story**)

Anything for Her Son (**free short story**)

Autism - novels and nonfiction:

Autism Goes to School

Autism Runs Away

Autism Belongs

Autism Talks and Talks

Autism Grows Up

Autism Goes to College

Autism Box Set

Autism Questions Parents Ask & the Answers They Seek

Autism Questions Teachers Ask & the Answers They Seek

ABOUT THE AUTHOR

Dr. Sharon A. Mitchell lives on a farm, with her nearest neighbor several miles away. Does that seem like a setting to spark the imagination? It does for her.

She takes long walks with her hundred-pound German Shepherd dogs, Pickles and Dill. (She didn't name them - don't blame her).

Her current projects are writing more books in the series The Farmers of Goodrich County - clean and wholesome romances with down-to-earth heroes, and heroines who are more than their match.

She's working on her eighth psychological thriller novel for the *When Bad Things Happen* series.

In addition to three short stories tied to that series, she's written six other novels, each featuring an autistic child or young adult. Two nonfiction books accompany that autism series.

Sharon's been a teacher, counselor, psychologist and consultant for decades and continues to teach university classes on kids who learn differently to soon-to-be teachers and administrators.

She loves to hear from her readers and always responds. Email her at sharon@sharonmitchellauthor.com.

bookbub.com/authors/sharon-a-mitchell

facebook.com/DrSharonAMitchell

twitter.com/AutismSite

instagram.com/autismsite

pinterest.com/mitchellsha3047